THE MASTER
OF
ILLUSION

THE DR. WILLIAM SCARLET MYSTERIES

Red Season

Year of the Rippers

THE MASTER OF ILLUSION

GARY GENARD

Cedar &
Maitland
Press

First Edition

Cover design: Llywellyn

Interior typesetting: Lorna Reid

ISBN: 978-1-7365556-8-2

Library of Congress Control Number: 2024909764

Printed in the United States of America

To order this book, please call (617) 993-3410 in the U.S., or contact info@garygenard.com. Group discounts are available.

Visit the author's website at www.garygenard.com

To Hilary Wood, Judith Gick, Valerie Colgan, and Francis Thomas.

And in memory of
The Webber Douglas Academy of Dramatic Art,
30/36 Clareville Street, South Kensington, London

Who is so deafe, or so blynde, as is hee, that wilfully will nother heare nor see?

— John Heywood (1546)

Mere impossibility is a consideration which, in magic, has no weight whatever.

— Nevil Maskelyne and David Devant, *Our Magic* (1911)

PROLOGUE

he sound was sharp, like something pointed striking wood.

From his position at the back of the nave in St Michael and All the Angels Church, the Rev. Charles Hathersley thought it came from the other end of the church near the altar. It was hard to say, though, because the twelfth-century building was notorious for echoing and magnifying every sound.

He listened, and heard it again. Yes, it seemed to come from just beyond the three-pointed Gothic arch that separated the nave from the altar. Was someone walking there?

The church was pitch black at 3.25 a.m.—the hour between three and four when the soul is most vulnerable and those who are weak die, thought the Reverend—for he hadn't bothered to turn on any of the gas lamps. He had been thinking that the dark was suited to his thoughts. But now he wished that something more than starlight were filtering through the arched side windows into the central space of the church.

Rev. Hathersley was afraid. Of an unrecognized sound in the dark, yes. But of something bigger than that, something he thought was coming. It was the reason he was up at this time of night or early morning, roaming the halls of the dark church like a ghost. Or scurrying like prey.

"By heaven, it won't help to think like *that*, Charlie," he told himself as he took his first steps down the center aisle toward the altar.

His fear had been hardly noticeable at first, a small cloud drifting across the sun. Then, over the course of just two weeks, it had grown into something that seemed to take all the light from the world. So that now in this darkness, it was at its strongest, weighing his shoulders down as he walked with a heavy sense of dread.

The interior of St Michael's was built with the natural acoustical materials of wood and stone pillars and arches, so that now it was his own footsteps that echoed throughout the nave. A newer church made of brick—he had seen them—would deaden sounds so that there wasn't this confusing echo. That would make things easier for him. But he knew that the way of an Anglican vicar is never meant to be easy.

His enemy wasn't a mystery to Rev. Hathersley—hadn't been even at the start two weeks ago, when he first realized he was in jeopardy. But this darkness put him too much at a disadvantage.

He would light some candles as soon as he reached the altar.

Approaching the front of the church with the pulpit on his left and the hymn board on his right, he could see the altar now. The fair linen cloth always present between services that included Holy Communion was there, as was the plain wooden cross, and the two tall gold candlesticks with candles at either end. In St Michael and All the Angels Church, the entire wall behind the altar was of stained glass, shaped in the form of the Gothic arches which led to it. So there was no room for the larger cross which some churches placed there.

As he passed the last of the dark wood pews, ready to walk up the two steps to the altar to light the candles, something to his left caught his eye. It was on the wall nearest to the pulpit.

He turned his head to look. When he saw what was there, logic compelled him to admit that either interior wall—to the left and right of the altar—were the only places where this could have been put.

It was at that moment that Rev. Charles Hathersley understood the fate that was in store for him.

The sharp sound he'd heard earlier came once more. This time, however, it was directly behind him.

CHAPTER 1

London Is Itself Again

Spring had come on once more, and London was reborn. The city felt its rebirth collectively and individually. Eighteen eighty-eight—Jack the Ripper's year—had been left behind in the bone-chilling cold of last November.

You felt coldest, thought William Scarlet as he watched the swans and ducks in the Hyde Park Serpentine, not in winter but in late autumn, when you've dressed too lightly to be out all day. Last summer and fall, it was as if London had been like that day after day, powerless against an inescapable cold fear that crept into its bones and stayed there.

But now the warm March sun of the spring of 1889 was shining. Cruel as it may be, it was pleasant to think that the horror of last year was a thing of the past. That certainly wasn't true concerning the tidal wave of articles, pamphlets, speeches, and books that had deluged London since the Ripper murders. Scarlet was sure those would continue for some time to come. But it was probably true in the minds of the people of London whose lives were already over-burdened by a daily struggle to survive.

Of course, the world would never know the truth about the five women who were murdered and carved up in awful fashion in Whitechapel, Spitalfields, and The City from August to November of last year. As far as London and the rest of the country were concerned, someone self-named "Jack the Ripper" had committed the crimes: a monster who had never been caught.

Only Scarlet and his friend Django Pierce-Jones knew about the vigilante group—the Friends of the Daughters of Night—that had really committed the murders of Mary Ann Nichols, Annie Chapman, Elizabeth Stride, Catherine Eddowes, and Mary Jane Kelly. And how each of the murderers had in turn suffered a savage retribution for their crimes.[*]

One day, perhaps, everyone else would know as well. That is, if The Society for Supernatural and Psychic Research that Scarlet and Pierce-Jones belonged to ever decided to open their files to the public.

At any rate, it wasn't Scarlet's concern.

Right now, the unseasonably warm March temperature and the springtime breezes were fine enough to crowd out any somber thoughts from a few months past. They made the blood race through Scarlet's veins, it seemed, for the first time in months.

"Wake up, doctor."

Scarlet looked up, but he was at a complete disadvantage. Whoever the woman was who had spoken, she was standing between the sun and the bench he was sitting on, so that he was looking up at nothing but a female silhouette. He leaned slightly to the left, and began to smile and stand at the same time.

"Miss Wilson. What an unexpected pleasure!"

"Are you sure you don't mean 'distraction,' Dr. Scarlet?" She wore a slightly mocking smile as they shook hands.

She was as striking as he remembered: a tall woman whose features immediately advertised both her attractiveness and intelligence. He remembered now her flawless rose complexion and naturally wavy auburn hair, which she still wore past her shoulders. Her eyes were just as large and dark, her eyebrows thin and arched in

---

[*] See Book 2 in the Dr. William Scarlet mystery series, *Year of the Rippers* (Cedar & Maitland Press, 2024).

the same way she had trimmed them previously. If her nose remained slightly too long, he didn't mind, for her generously wide mouth made the proportions pleasing.

This was Catherine Wilson. She was the older sister of Elizabeth Wilson, whose fiancé at the time, Ambrose Reed, had been the target of a dangerous demonic possession which Scarlet had helped uncover and defeat a year and a half ago. Reed had recovered well, and from everything Scarlet had heard since then, had reclaimed his position as London's most in-demand young painter.

Scarlet guessed Catherine's age at a year or so less than his own thirty-four—unusual for a not-yet-married woman in English society. He put it down to her intelligence and boldness of personality. Together, they probably scared away the not remotely equal suitors that would be available to her.

He released his hand from her firm grasp and indicated the now-empty bench.

"Please," he said, adding: "That is, do you have a moment?"

She had on a full-length velvet-like hooped skirt in what Scarlet would call a rich Russian Blue; a black ladies jacket that came to three-quarters length on her arms; and black ankle boots. Had the weather been colder, she probably would have been carrying a muff the same color as the jacket, and a bonnet of some kind, though now her head was bare.

It was a simple and elegant outfit, and he noted it in particular because of the way Catherine Wilson sat down while wearing it. She did it the way women of breeding manage it—moving effortlessly from the standing position to the sitting one while remaining straight as a ramrod the entire time. She took a deep breath, closed her eyes and turned her face to the sun.

"'Daffodils, that come before the swallow dares, and take the winds of March with beauty.'"

"Shakespeare, *The Winter's Tale*."

"Very good, Doctor!" she said, lowering her head to look at him where he sat beside her.

"Even though there's no wind today."

"Well, there's that," said Catherine Wilson, laughing.

"You're looking wonderful, madam," he said, hoping that he sounded as sincere as he was. "If anything, younger by a year or two since I last saw you. How do you manage it, Miss Wilson?"

"If anything, sir, addressing me as 'madam,' and 'Miss Wilson,' makes me sound ancient! I insist you call me Catherine . . . that is, if I may address you as William?"

"You may. All right, Catherine. But my question remains: how do you manage it?"

"It's all illusion, William. I mostly employ angles and mirrors to my benefit."

"What? Out in the open like this?"

"Ah! You're obviously not used to seeing a master at work, sir."

He bowed his head, placing his hand on his breast. "I concede the point." He smiled. "And how are your sister and her husband?"

"Deliriously happy. Mr. and Mrs. Reed are expecting, you see."

"That's marvelous!" said Scarlet, who hadn't heard the news.

"I assure you they are both quite wonderful," said Catherine. "Thanks to you."

Scarlet responded as one does to such a statement. He lowered his head slightly, smiled a tight smile, and said nothing.

"And what about you? Your practice, and your work at Scotland Yard. Are they going well?"

"They are. We're as busy as ever, you may be sure."

There was no need to mention the fallout from the Ripper investigation of last year, which had consumed not only the Metropolitan Police/Scotland Yard, but the City of London force as well, and continued to be a black eye for the Home Office. And of course, he could never share the truth about the murders which his own investigation and that of Pierce-Jones had uncovered.

Turning their bodies slightly toward one another on the bench, the two exchanged the polite inquiries which are part of a chance meeting like this one:

- How are your parents? [This referred to Mr. Hiram Wilson, Head of the Railway Department, and his wife Margaret.]

- And your good friend, that dashing gentleman, Django Pierce-Jones?

- My time? Well, I'm teaching a course as demonstrator of anatomy at St George's Hospital. Yes, I'm enjoying it immensely. . . . Are you enjoying the start of the Season?

- Oh, yes. And you? Have you attended the dance or the theatre? (She didn't think he was the opera type, so she didn't include it.)

"Have you seen the latest sensation?" she asked now.

He looked at her blankly. He hadn't a clue of what she meant.

"I'm afraid not. What is the latest sensation?"

"The magicians, of course. And the fierce rivalry between the two greatest of them!"

Scarlet shook his head while shrugging his shoulders. Catherine Wilson took his meaning immediately.

"You *are* spending too much time in your anatomy room, or whatever it's called," she scolded him. "Don't you know that this is the season of magic in London? It's simply everywhere." Her tone had a mocking quality.

"Sorry," he said, though he wasn't. "I must have missed it."

"You certainly appear to have done so! If you had read the society columns, you'd know that it began last year. There's been considerable interest here and on the continent in spiritualism because of the stage shows of the Fox Sisters and the Davenport Brothers in America. Spirit cabinets and all of that. . . . Surely you've heard of the spiritualist movement?"

"Of course," he replied. And he had. He simply hadn't had the time to follow any of it closely. Anyway, Pierce-Jones, who was a true medium, would be much more familiar with the phenomenon than he was.

"Then you must know that a few years ago, stage magicians began exposing the trickery involved in the spiritualist performances. Well, who better?"

"What's the difference, then?"

"You mean between the spiritualism shows and the magicians?"

"Exactly."

"Well, as I understand it, magicians always claim that their illusions are 'honest'—that they use conjuring tricks purely for entertainment. Magic for magic's sake, as it were. They say it's only the frauds who claim to have true spiritual powers. And it appears to be working. The spiritualist movement is on the wane. People seem to like the fact that magic tricks are all illusion. They know it's impossible, yet want it to happen right in front of their eyes every night."

"And this has created a craze in the London theatres?"

"In some of the theatres, but mostly in the music halls and on the variety stages. That, and the rivalries that have sprung up as to which magician features the best act. Some of the stage effects have become quite elaborate. People are now going from one music hall or theatre to another, to see which magician has outdone the other with the latest grand illusion.

"Do you see, then," she concluded in the same matter-of-fact tone, "how your dedication to the advancement of science has made you miss out on this stupendous turn of events?" She picked up on his own earlier thought and said: "I'll bet your friend, Mr. Pierce-Jones, knows all about it, and has probably seen some of it."

"No doubt. What is the rivalry between the two greatest magicians that you mentioned?"

"Oh. There's a very public competition going on between Max von Leiden, who is known as 'The Master of Illusion,' and Giuseppe Caliosto, who calls himself 'Marco the Magnificent.'"

"I must say, it sounds like an earth-shattering battle."

"You may mock, Doctor, but the season is abuzz with the tit-for-tat performances by the two of them. In fact, these two gentlemen attract enough crowds that they are regularly booked into the theatres rather than the music halls. Herr Von Leiden is currently enjoying an eight-week run at the Queen Victoria Theatre

Royal, and Signor Caliosto recently opened a gala show at Covent Garden."

Scarlet knew that those two theatres were, in fact, major venues.

"Live and learn," he admitted defeat. "It appears you're right . . . I have been missing out. Thank you for—"

"Bringing you back from the dead?" Catherine Wilson said before he could finish, and stood.

Scarlet laughed.

"As to that, I refuse to comment," he said, rising in his turn. "It does me good to see you, Catherine," he added spontaneously.

"And me you, William," she replied.

They shook hands warmly, this time in departure.

CHAPTER 2

A Stupendous World of Magic

t is remarkably easy for a medical doctor to spend all of his time with sick and injured people, in consultations with colleagues, and attending to patients in hospital. For a police surgeon, the autopsy suite in the sub-basement of Scotland Yard at No. 5, Whitehall Place, Westminster, was simply another version of the same Venus Fly Trap.

Scarlet had been thinking along these lines since his conversation with Catherine Wilson in Hyde Park.

Back from the dead, indeed.

It was springtime, and attendance at a pair of shows performed by rival master magicians seemed in order. No, more than in order—absolutely necessary!

Scarlet had been interested in amateur theatrics his whole life, and had performed in the school dramatic clubs at Enfield Academy in North London and at Balliol College, Oxford. One day from that time still stood out vividly in his memory, in fact. It had been an outing with some friends from the academy and three girls from the neighboring country girls' school who had been drafted for the boys' school's play.

The group had come upon a fair, set up on nearby Bentley Heath. Seeing it, one of the girls had remarked: "A fair was the last thing I expected to find today. But now, attending one is the only thing in the world I want to do!"

Scarlet had been struck by the remark that day, and it had stayed with him. It seemed to sum up the actor's personality: the ability to immerse oneself wholly in an imaginary world at the drop of a hat— and the more fantastical that world, the better.

It was how he felt now about attending a magic show. There would be criminal cases and autopsies enough tomorrow and the day after that. In the meantime, he felt that his soul needed to breathe, as much as his lungs hungered for the spring air after winter.

His morning sessions with patients at the surgery in his home in Chelsea were finished, and his administrative load wasn't burdensome at the moment. He could leave Whitehall, return home to change, and meet Django Pierce-Jones for dinner at Scarlet's club, the Athenaeum, at 8.00 as planned.

"I WANT YOU TO tell me about the magicians' shows currently in London," he said to Pierce-Jones after they'd shaken hands and sat down in the Athenaeum's dining room. "And whatever you know about the spiritualists' shows."

Django look at his friend steadily.

He said: "I was thinking of the sole. Or . . ." (a quick look back at the menu) "perhaps the leg of lamb. What do you suggest?"

"All right, bastard," replied Scarlet with a grin. "Sorry. Let's order."

The food was always exceptional at the Athenaeum, and Pierce-Jones probably would have preferred to sample more of it before he finally replied to Scarlet's comments of the last few minutes.

"Catherine's absolutely right," he said. "Tickets to the magic shows are the hottest items in London right now. Especially those of von Leiden and Caliosto, who have developed quite a rivalry."

"So I understand," said Scarlet. "And what's so special about these two?"

Pierce-Jones smiled, took a sip of Brunello di Montalcino,[*] and leaned back in his forest-green tufted dining chair.

"They are the greatest of the greatest—the *crème de la crème*—at least in their own minds. Truth be told, they are both spectacular magicians. They recently developed a rivalry that has each of them trying to over-top the other in remarkable illusions, sometimes on the same night. It's a wonder they're not blasting each other with magic wands from opposite street corners in the theatre district. Fortunately, one of them performs at the Queen Victoria Theatre Royal in Haymarket, and the other in Covent Garden."

"That's only a half-mile's distance from each other."

"Well, it's a sight better than if Caliosto weren't at Covent Garden but at Her Majesty's Theatre, which is just across the damned street from the Theatre Royal where von Leiden is appearing."

It always amused Scarlet to hear Pierce-Jones employ a British gentleman's expressions. 'Damned street,' indeed!

Scarlet wasn't convinced. "Mightn't a famous public rivalry be just another trick to fill the house?"

"I don't think so," replied Django. "I believe it's personal. There have been comments, for instance, that have revealed considerable animosity."

"Fair enough," said Scarlet, tucking into his food again. "All right, then. Tell me about these two great magicians."

"Well, you know that practically every magician uses 'Famous,' 'Extraordinary,' 'Amazing,' and so on before their name, right?"

"Of course."

"And someone is always declaring he has 'The World's Greatest

---

[*] A red wine from the hill town of Montalcino in Tuscany, known for being aged for over a decade in wood barrels. The wine was introduced on the international market the previous year. The Athenaeum, one of the premier London gentlemen's clubs, benefits from the fact that one of the members of The Society for Supernatural and Psychic Research that Scarlet and Pierce-Jones belong to is Enzo Conti, vintner and importer of renowned wines from Italy.

Magic Show.' But these two are different. They're not only both exceptional conjurers in performance. They both excel at creating extraordinary stage illusions. Actually, that's not a surprise where one of them is concerned."

"Who?"

"Giuseppe Caliosto—who bills himself as Marco the Magnificent. His father was a cabinet-maker, and taught his son the art. Did you know that most magicians come from a family background of either watchmaking or cabinet-making?"

"No, I didn't. But it makes perfect sense."

"Of course, it does," agreed Pierce-Jones. "Most of the big illusions in a magician's act depend upon mechanical design more than anything."

"Such as the disappearing cabinet?"

"Absolutely. Despite the name, it's the person inside who disappears, of course, not the cabinet.

"Incidentally," Django added, "there's your link to the spiritualists' acts you asked about. The spirit cabinet featured by the Americans the Davenport Brothers in the 1850s was a very famous conjuring act. The brothers were tied hand and foot and placed in a locked cabinet with an assortment of musical instruments. Once the cabinet door was closed and locked, music would begin to play, bells would ring, and so on, apparently all of it produced on those instruments.

"At some point in the midst of all this, the cabinet door would be unlocked and opened by an assistant. The brothers could be seen inside, still securely tied. Supposedly, spirits from the Great Beyond were producing the music. It was all part of the Spiritualism mania which gripped America, starting with the Fox Sisters' first public performance in 1849."

"And people believed in these invisible musicians?"

"Of course. They were Americans."

Pierce-Jones waited for Scarlet to finish laughing.

"Actually, it wasn't long before well-known magicians in

Europe and America started debunking the Davenports' act and demonstrating how the tricks were really accomplished. Your man Caliosto was one of the principal debunkers, by the way."

"But why would fellow conjurers reveal the secrets of magic illusions?"

"Ah—a very pretty question," replied Pierce-Jones. "Evidently, it's a point of honor for them. Professional magicians don't want people to think they possess supernatural abilities. You can see how easily that could be the case, since they seem to suspend or contradict natural laws as if they had extraordinary powers. They openly admit that they are what they call honest conjurers, who perform illusions solely for entertainment. Only the dishonest and charlatans claim otherworldly powers."

"Catherine said the same thing," Scarlet admitted. "Apparently, people hold on to their illusions."

"Are you sure you don't mean delusions? Magicians are master psychologists, my friend."

Scarlet didn't want to go down that road at the moment.

"Does Caliosto—Marco the Magnificent—still make the exposure of spiritualism part of his act?" he asked.

"No, that's old hat now," replied Django. "The best stage acts are those that keep coming up with new illusions. Sometimes that means building on the tricks of rivals, or coming up with entirely new effects."

"And what is Marco the Magnificent known for now?"

"Well, he's accomplished at all of the major illusions that most of the masters perform these days. But he's best known for The Bullet Catch."

"What in the world is that?"

"It's just what it sounds like," replied Pierce-Jones. "A volunteer from the audience fires a rifle point-blank at the magician. Sometimes, it's a firing squad dressed in military uniforms. If it's one individual firing the weapon, he or she inspects the round beforehand and daubs it with a bit of paint . . . they're always real bullets, incidentally. If it's a firing squad, the audience volunteer hands the bullets to the marksmen. It's apparently an article of faith among magicians that this audience volunteer is never a plant. The rifle or rifles are then fired at the magician from just a few feet away, and he catches the bullet or all of them in one hand. Sometimes, he catches a single bullet in his teeth."

"What!"

"I'm not exaggerating, old boy. That's exactly the way it's done."

"Extraordinary," said Scarlet. "Is it considered dangerous?"

"As far as I can tell, it *is* dangerous," replied Django. "But defying death has always been part of the attraction of great magicians' shows."

"I should say," agreed Scarlet.

Dessert and coffee had come by then, and the two men attended to it, still considering, perhaps, the implications of The Bullet Catch. Finally, Scarlet asked:

"And what about Max von Leiden?"

"'The Master of Illusion,'" answered Django. "He's an entirely different kettle of fish from Marco the Magnificent. To begin with, he's really German, not a made-up stage German. His stage act is called *Phantasmagoria*. Marco's, incidentally, is called *The Cabalistic Laboratory*."

"What's von Leiden's show like?"

"Much darker than Caliosto's. In fact, von Leiden has a much more mysterious persona. He looks the part, for one thing—he's very tall, with dark hair and a peaked hairline, black moustaches and a goatee, and large, arching eyebrows. His fingers are extraordinarily long and delicate. He has a reputation for going beyond traditional magic, for pushing the boundaries of nature and manipulating human psychology."

"How does he do such a thing?"

"I honestly don't know, Will. You'll have to attend a show and report back."

"Indeed, I'll do that. What's he known for? Aside from playing the mysterious dark stranger, I mean?"

Django Pierce-Jones thought about his answer.

"It's an odd thing," he said. "He apparently grants people's wishes."

"You must be joking."

"I'm not. I really don't know much about it, but apparently it's true. The claim, I mean. I understand it's a special part of his act—one he performs only occasionally. I hear there's no knowing beforehand whether he will be performing it that night with a volunteer from the audience."

"All the more reason for people to flock to his shows, I would think," said Scarlet. "Not knowing whether this will be the night, I mean."

"It would certainly have that effect, wouldn't it?" said Django.

He looked at his friend closely.

"There's a spark in your eye, old man," he said. "I believe you'd like to get to the bottom of what's going on in these remarkable illusions." And he quoted: "'I see you stand like greyhounds in the slips, straining upon the start.'"

Scarlet thought about that.

"I think you're right," he said. "I have the time at the moment, and it does sound intriguing. . . . Yes—the game's afoot," concluded Scarlet, who after all knew his Shakespeare at least as well as Pierce-Jones.

CHAPTER 3

Enough To Catch Your Death

arco the Magnificent's *Cabalistic Laboratory* was the easier of the two shows to obtain tickets for—slightly. Still, the pair of seats in the immense Covent Garden was in the slips or fourth level, and all the way over on stage right.

Scarlet had decided to invite Catherine Wilson. It would be pleasant to see her again, and her sharp intelligence made her the perfect companion to view a magic show. They met at the theatre rather than for dinner beforehand. (Scarlet was so intent on seeing one of the magic shows he'd been missing out on that he hadn't even thought of an invitation to dinner.)

Catherine wore what Scarlet thought was a magnificent dress, of a shade between lapis and azure blue, with a floral print and barely visible white vertical stripes. The bodice hugged her waist tightly (surely she was wearing a corset), before flaring out to the sides and back. The front of the dress featured not one but two skirts—the outer one rounded with a curved, scalloped design alternating light and dark blue fabric at the bottom, the inner skirt showing the same design and colors but with a straight cut. The three-quarters sleeves had an abundance of white lace which became the cuffs.

He was just about to comment on the dress but caught himself before making that mistake.

"You look smashing!" he said instead.

Catherine's eyes sparkled, and she showed just the slightest hint of raising her shoulders. The gesture seemed to say, "Yes, it is fun to dress up for the theatre!" That was much better than accepting the compliment as her due as some women did; or worse, displaying the trite body language of false modesty which was so popular.

She took his arm and said: "Just don't raise your hand for me if he asks for volunteers. I'd turn getting up the stairs with this dress into a comedy which would ruin the entire performance!"

"Agreed," said Scarlet with a smile. "And kindly turn my face toward the stage now and then if I keep looking at you."

Catherine laughed, and replied: "I see I made the right decision in accepting your invitation, sir."

Even from this high up, the scale and opulence of the scenic design was striking. The compensation for them in terms of their seating, was that although they were sitting in the fourth level, the curvature of the balcony meant that they were actually close to the stage, even if they had to view it from an extreme angle.

It occurred to Scarlet that they might be able to see something taking place behind the magician's back that the audience directly in front of him wouldn't be aware of. He dismissed the thought immediately, however. The purveyors of a first-class magic act would know the sight-lines from every seat in the house, even one as large and grand as Covent Garden. Nothing would be left to chance in terms of any audience member noticing something they shouldn't be seeing. Also, of course, any great magician is a master of misdirection. So he told himself to just sit back and enjoy the show.

Marco the Magnificent had chosen the exotic East as the theme and locale of his act, and everything on stage reflected that motif. The stage floor was painted in an intricate colorful pattern of squares, diamonds, and crescents. The back wall was painted in a *trompe l'oeil* scene of red-and-white Moorish arches that looked out on variously-shaped minarets, domes, and towers. Gas lights shaped like giant oil-lamps from a genii tale hung from a real ceiling; and drapes adorned with Eastern colors and designs curved down from the ceiling at a variety of angles to add to the vaguely Arabian setting. Already, the strong scent of incense wafted outward from the stage, filling the house.

As Scarlet looked down at this spectacle, he realized that the entire set was enclosed within a giant black box. And he remembered a comment Django had made, that some magicians insist in their contracts on "boxing" their set. The idea was that if other magicians found (or bribed) their way backstage, they wouldn't be able to discover any magical secrets in terms of machinery or effects.

The house lights slowly dimmed, the audience hushed, and the show began.

While Eastern music swelled from somewhere with a flute's distinctive quavers, the back wall of the stage set parted, like the gates of a medieval city. Gliding silently forward onto the stage appeared a smaller set, a room also decorated in exotic furnishings.

This was clearly the working space of a master wizard. On a long table at stage right sat a collection of experimental equipment: tall glass decanters filled with different colored liquids and with crystal stoppers; oversized (presumably so they were visible from the back of the house) ceramic mortars and pestles; and a magician's wands scattered around carelessly. Two glass globes that glowed mysteriously—one blue, the other orange—sat at each end of the table. Here and there, ancient-looking books were opened to pages featuring exotic lettering. This was obviously The Cabalistic Laboratory.

In the middle of the laboratory stood a heavyset man dressed in a fantastical white-and-gold outfit with hugely billowing trousers. He wore a white turban with an enormous "ruby" set front-and-center, and sparkling black slippers that curved up at the toes, Aladdin-like. Clearly, this was Marco the Magnificent, looking every inch the part.

The fact that this outfit, and the entire setting, sprung more from a costumer and stage designer's imagination than anything that had ever existed didn't matter. As far as the audience was concerned, they were about to witness the secrets of The Cabalistic Laboratory: a conjurer's domain that had explored—and now brought to Europe—the vast mysteries of the East!

And what was wrong with that? thought Scarlet. A magician's job above all else is to entertain. Marco had simply built his show with that directive in mind. A quick glance at Catherine, in fact, showed her eyes wide open with a look of anticipatory delight.

Marco now strode to the very edge of his inner "room" closest to the audience. He showed both his hands, which were empty. Then he raised his right hand high above his head and positioned his left hand, curled as if to catch something, below his waist. Suddenly, a golden waterfall of coins began cascading from his raised hand into the hand that awaited them. Then he hurled the golden doubloons into the audience. As people close to the stage cupped their hands to receive them, in mid-air the coins turned into gold confetti, which floated down harmlessly into their laps. The audience immediately broke into applause.

"Ladies and gentlemen, welcome!" said Marco the Magnificent, in a voice that was surprisingly thin. Scarlet saw Catherine unconsciously shift her body forward, to better catch the words spoken by that voice, so far below them.

"For thousands of years," he continued, "enchanters in the exotic realms of the East have practiced their craft, creating wonders beyond our understanding. But little by little, the secrets to these mysteries have become known in the West, by those brave enough to uncover them and bring them back.

"For decades, I have searched and gathered and searched some more. Tonight, I have brought these wonders to share with you—in The Cabalistic Laboratory!"

[Applause]

The voice dropped to a low pitch and became serious.

"For those of you who are faint of heart or with a medical

condition, I urge you to leave at the interval. The second half of our show will feature the death-defying Bullet Catch—the illusion that is no illusion—and which uses real gunpowder and actual bullets. These bullets will be inspected by one of you and marked before they are loaded into the rifles. Ladies and gentlemen . . . I will *catch* those bullets after they are fired from the rifles! That's for the second half of the show. Once again, my friends, I suggest you leave before that point if this dangerous experiment will cause you distress."

[Smattering of uncertain applause]

"But first . . . The Cabalistic Laboratory!"

What followed was a progression of illusions typical of a first-class magic act of the age: sleight-of-hand featuring card tricks, then coins; cups and balls tricks; disappearances and reappearances involving handkerchiefs; a dove in a cage that miraculously escaped its confinement while the cage itself vanished, and so on. All of these standard magic ploys were given an oriental flavor by Marco's banter; by the exotic patterns painted or printed on the fabrics and other materials used; and by the harem-like attire of the two female assistants.

More amazing displays of legerdemain followed. Each one was accompanied by an attractive female assistant, who crossed the stage while holding a placard announcing the name of the trick:

"The Top-Hat": A man's top hat, borrowed from a spectator brought on stage, was flourished by Marco and turned toward the audience to show that it was empty. While crossing the stage to return it, however, the magician discovered that the hat seemed unnaturally heavy, and he had the hat's owner feel its weight as well. Attempting to dislodge what was inside the hat by shaking it mightily with the opening downward, the magician finally succeeded—as a cannonball fell onto the stage and rolled into the wings with a mighty rumbling sound.

"The Demolished Watch": Marco asked for a volunteer who owned a pocket-watch. Standing next to the man onstage, Marco examined the watch and announced that it was running slow. Before the owner could protest, the magician placed the watch in a mortar and proceeded to smash and grind it to bits with a pestle. He tipped the mortar so that the now-worthless remains of the watch poured into the hands of the astonished audience volunteer. When the man, after looking at the pile of useless metal he held, demanded his timepiece back, Marco considered the request, nodded, and produced—apparently from inside his coat—a loaf of bread which he placed on the table. Then he transferred the rattling remains of the watch into the barrel of a revolver (announcing to the audience that this wasn't the gun to be used later in The Bullet Catch), and aimed and fired the weapon at the bread. He then tore the loaf in half with his hands, revealing the watch hidden inside the bread. The amazed volunteer declared that this was his watch, as pristine as when the trick began!

"The Pickpocket": A humorous episode involved a gentleman brought on stage, whom Marco promptly and invisibly (to the man at least) relieved of his wallet. He confessed the theft immediately, however, producing the wallet; and while the fellow was examining it (quickly counting the money inside, surely), Marco removed the man's eyeglasses and placed them on his own head. A brief discussion followed, with Marco looking at the man through his own glasses! The gentleman was returning to his seat, still unaware of what had happened, until Marco called to him with the glasses in his hand.

It was all delightful. The magician showed the boldness and audacity of all master conjurers, and the applause was frequent. Scarlet and Catherine were as grateful as everyone else for being consistently deluded (and entertained).

An entr'acte followed featuring Marie Lloyd, the enormously popular music hall performer. Scarlet, no fan of class distinctions, was amused to hear the Cockney singer give her rendition of "She Sits Among the Cabbages and Peas," the song whose risqué title had for the past few months been outraging Laura Ormiston Chant and members of the Social Purity Alliance.

WHEN THE DRURY LANE'S scarlet curtain rose for the second act, the audience saw that The Cabalistic Laboratory had disappeared. The stage was completely open now, with only *trompe l'oeil* paintings on the back wall of Moorish arches and an Arabian city in the background.

Scarlet knew that the most spectacular illusions of a magic show took place in the second half. But even when elaborate machinery was brought on stage (there was none here now), it was always the control of a master magician at work that raised a show from a series of parlour tricks to an art form.

At first, Marco the Magnificent created modest but striking illusions.

He transformed a seed into an orange tree in a pot which grew steadily to a height of three feet and *bore actual fruit*. Assuring the spectators that the fruit was real, he cut one of the oranges open with a knife, and tossed others into the audience.

Next, a placard on a stand was placed on stage by one of the female assistants.

It read:

Simultaneously, with the help of a dolly, the other assistant wheeled a small round table onstage. Marco now stood behind this table with a shawl draped over his shoulders.

"Gentlemen," he began, projecting his small voice as much as he could to the packed house. "As in all things, I am here at your service. Now that the weather is turning milder, which of us . . . and you too, ladies (widening his outspread arms further) . . . would not enjoy a day in the countryside in the fresh air? And some of us, I am sure, would delight in spending such a day fishing. Is that not so?"

Sounds of approbation in male tones from different parts of the house.

"Now, the fishing rod may be the preferred piece of equipment in this endeavour. But what a nuisance! The *net*, gentlemen, is far superior. And here is ours!"

The magician now swept the shawl off his shoulder and held it before the audience. "You will see that there is nothing inside this cloth—excuse me, this *net*—on one side or the other." The 'net' was turned around so that both sides can be seen. "Pay attention, ladies and gentlemen, for the magic is about to begin. Imagine that this small round table is a favorite fishing spot . . . we will call it 'The Magic Fish Pond.' I now walk all the way around the pond, looking into the water. Are there any fish in the pond today?" Marco was back to his starting place now. "I cast my net . . ."

He threw the empty cloth into the air and allowed it to float down to cover the table.

"Let us see!"

The conjurer grabbed hold of one corner of the cloth, and in a quick and fluid movement, draped it across the front of the table then pulled it away. Resting on the bare table was a fish bowl—a good 10 inches in diameter—filled to the brim with water and containing four fish, swimming merrily!

A deep bow acknowledged the loud applause at the impossible result.

"At this time, I must ask your indulgence," Marco next informed the audience. "We must take a brief pause while we prepare for the evening's final entertainment—The Bullet Catch. If you will kindly wait patiently for only a short time, we must assemble the additional cast necessary for this dangerous experiment."

With a final bow, Marco backed up past the line of the proscenium arch, and the curtain came down. Ten minutes later, it rose again.

The tableau that greeted the audience this time was ceremonial, and grim. Slightly to the right of mid-stage from the spectators' point of view stood Marco the Magnificent, now dressed in a humble (and again vaguely Arabian) prison outfit.

Facing him at a distance of perhaps ten feet, stood a squad of six Ottoman-looking soldiers and an officer. The military men were dressed in bright blue single-breasted uniforms with gold buttons, except for the officer, whose jacket was double-breasted. All of the men wore red fezzes with gold tassels, and the officer had gold epaulets.

The men stood at attention in a line facing Marco: the squad of six enlisted men holding the rifles at their right hip with the stocks resting on the stage floor, the officer with the obligatory sword in a scabbard at his side. Midway between the soldiers and Marco stood one of the female assistants, looking uneasy.

When sufficient time had passed for the spectators to take in this scene, Marco turned toward the audience and took a step forward.

"And now, ladies and gentlemen, our final experiment of the evening. Once again, I will attempt the impossible: to catch a bullet fired from a rifle at point-blank range! *Six* of them, in fact! Bear in mind my friends, what you are about to see is carried out with real bullets, fired with actual gunpowder from working military rifles.

"I must ask for complete silence to prepare for this dangerous undertaking." A slight tilt of the head. "A poor choice of word, I'm afraid. However," and the tone became serious again: "As you will see, this demonstration is entirely real, with no fakery involved whatsoever.

"We will begin. May I have a volunteer from the audience?"

As the house lights came up, men's hands, and here and there a woman's, rose into the air. Marco stepped further downstage closer to the audience, and scanned the house, concentrating. But he did not make a choice of volunteer. The tension rose, and Scarlet recognized it all as a master stroke of showmanship. Naturally Marco would be extraordinarily careful concerning who he chose. It was well known that a volunteer playing a prank, or an enemy of the magician, might place their own bullet in the barrel of the gun, and that men had died as a result of such treachery. Finally, with an almost imperceptible nod, the man in prison garb pointed to what looked like the exact center of the downstairs stalls.

"You, sir!" he bellowed, his voice unexpectedly strong. "Kindly come up on stage."

The fellow was in late middle-age, small and round and balding, dressed in a checkered brown suit and carrying a bowler hat. He was decidedly a working man, and whether that was part of Marco's decision none knew, but all wondered. The little man's demeanor was serious and respectful as he made his way up the side stairs to center-stage. As he did, a harem-dressed assistant came forward so that she was just upstage of him, with her arm outstretched and something in the palm of her hand.

Marco stepped forward to meet the man, so that the three of them formed a triangle on stage. The magician took whatever it was in the girl's hand and brandished it in a cupped palm so that the entire audience could see.

"Six real bullets, ladies and gentlemen." He turned to the volunteer. "Would you kindly verify this, sir?"

Marco handed them to the other man, who appeared to examine each one closely. Then the assistant gave him a dish and a small painter's brush.

"Would you, sir," said Marco, "kindly mark an 'X' on each of the lead portions of the bullets with this red paint?"

When that was done, the magician said: "Would you now please give the bullets to my assistant?"

She held out her hand, and the volunteer did so.

"And now, sir," announced Marco, "the rifles."

The soldiers stepped forward, and one by one each handed his rifle to the man in the brown suit. Whether the audience volunteer was a military veteran or not, he appeared to be familiar with such weapons. He hefted each rifle in turn, opened and closed the bolt actions, and without tilting the barrel too close in each case, glanced obliquely into the muzzles to see if they were clear. Then he nodded firmly and handed the weapons back to the soldiers.

Marco the Magnificent asked the volunteer if he was satisfied with the inspection, and the man said that he was. The assistant handed a bullet to each soldier. With a characteristically loud noise that was magnified by six, the shells were rammed into the firing chambers by the bolt action of the rifles.

The small gathering on stage now took up their final positions. The girl led the gentleman volunteer far upstage where he would be safe, and Marco turned to face the soldiers and officers. By this time, the group had formed into the straight line of a firing squad. Six rifles now pointed at the magician at a distance of perhaps ten feet.

The officer stood stiffly at attention. From somewhere backstage, a snare drum began a dramatic tattoo.

"Ready . . . aim . . . *FIRE!*"

The rifles roared. When the audience opened their eyes after the involuntary blink response, they saw Marco with his right arm outstretched, grasping something in his fist. He spun toward the audience and raised his arm above his head, opening his fist and expertly cupping his hand so that all could see what was in them without the objects falling out onstage.

He was holding six pieces of lead—each one still perfectly formed into its tapered shape since none of them had passed through anything but air. For everyone seated in the stalls, at least, a painted red "X" was clearly visible on each one.

The audience had leaped to its feet. Thunderous applause and shouts of "Bravo!" "Here, here!" and "Bloody hell!," filled the huge house of Covent Garden.

Scarlet and Catherine were on their feet with the rest.

All around them people were laughing and shouting acclamations. They heard a man nearby proclaim loudly (and this wit's accent wasn't refined in the least):

"Ha! Ha! It's enough to make you catch your bleedin' death!"

CHAPTER 4

A Disease Like No Other

As master magicians like Marco the Magnificent would be the first to admit, the world of magic isn't the world of reality. And so the day after The Cabalistic Laboratory show, and the rest of that week, was filled for Scarlet with the normal duties of an assistant chief surgeon of the Metropolitan Police, or as the force was more popularly known: Scotland Yard.

Among Scarlet's work-related activities that week:

* Examining twenty-three individuals who, for whatever misguided reasons, were intent on joining the 12,000 members of the Metropolitan Police. In the medical examination, the police surgeon was concerned with the following characteristics:

- Under thirty-five years of age.
- Sound in mind and body.
- If married, with no more than two children.
- Minimum height of 5 feet and 7 inches.
- Eyesight good (both eyes).
- Able to read and write.
- Willing to be vaccinated (which happened immediately upon acceptance).

* A careful reading of the Post Mortem Examination and Case Books of hospitals within the Metropolitan Police divisions for all cases of homicide, suicide, accidental, and unexplained death.

* Surgery in a case of "a penetrating wound of the thorax and abdomen" (stabbing) that had occurred in Blunts Lane, in Eltham in southeast London. Two boys had disturbed a man walking with a female companion. The man, who was drunk, chased one of the boys and stabbed him in the back with a small folding knife. The knife had penetrated the lung but was broken against one of the ribs, leaving a piece of the blade in the lung. Scarlet operated successfully to remove the fragment.

*Three autopsies—all performed at the request of hospitals whose own medical staffs were over-burdened with post-mortem examinations: (1) A 44-year-old labourer who suffered a fatal clot in the subdural space opposite the 9th and 10th dorsal vertebrae. (2) The wife of a verger or lay minister, 45 years old, who had been operated on for a strangulated umbilical hernia and succumbed to intestinal gas gangrene four days later. (3) A 12-year-old boy with suspected Bright's Disease (*albuminuria* or chronic disease of the kidney), confirmed upon autopsy.

In addition, there was an odd case from Scarlet's small private practice in his surgery at his home in Chelsea. The female patient, whom he hadn't seen previously, appeared to be in her mid-seventies. She exhibited the normal appearance of someone her age. Her face was well-lined, with the typical loss of skin elasticity. Her nose was prominent—perhaps due to the gauntness of her cheeks—and the mouth was turned downward, with age-characteristic wrinkles all around it.

More interesting to Scarlet was the pronounced erythema on the cheeks: an inflammatory blush that had the appearance of broken capillaries. But Scarlet didn't think that was the cause of the rash. The German ophthalmologist, August von Rothmund had described a condition in the late 1860s that included this facial feature. But Rothmund–Thomson syndrome, as it came to be known, featured other prominent deficits, including bone defects, that were not evident here. Her grey hair clung to her scalp limply and without luster.

The woman's name, as given to him by his assistant, was Mrs. Walter Keeley-Campbell. And her style of dress seemed calculated to give exactly the opposite impression from that conveyed by her physical appearance. She wore a voluminous lime-green hat with a huge white ostrich feather, a powder-blue dress with matching shoes, and was carrying a pink parasol. It seemed a transparent attempt to appear younger, or fresher, or *something* other than who and what she was. Whatever her intentions, however, Scarlet's concern was the state of her health. And so, the standard first question.

"What is your complaint, madam?" he began.

"You mustn't mis-name me, doctor," came the surprising and immediate reply. "I am widowed, so you may call me 'Miss.'" Scarlet took a second or two to realize that the woman wasn't joking, and tried again.

"Why have you come to see me?"

His patient thought for a moment, sadly, it seemed to him.

"Ennui, doctor. Weariness, loss of desire. Perhaps a physician would call it melancholia. Am I correct that your father was Dr. James Scarlet, the well-known alienist?"

"Yes, that's true," Scarlet answered. "He preferred the term psychiatric doctor, however."

"Not 'psychiatrist'?"

"He hated that term, actually."

She laughed. The sound was dry and scratchy.

"And do you specialize in the same area? Aside from your position with the police, I mean."

"I do not, Mrs.— I'm sorry. Is it 'Miss Keeley,' then?"

"Yes, thank you. Miss Harriet Keeley."

"Do I understand from your question that you are here due to complaints of the mind?"

"No. Not at all. I was simply curious. And the fact is, doctor, I do suffer from melancholy. But my complaints, as you call them, are decidedly physical in nature, and have led to my melancholia. Do you see?"

"Yes, of course. And what are your physical complaints, mad— Miss Keeley?"

"Everything."

"I'm afraid I don't understand."

"How old would you say I am, Doctor?"

Scarlet smiled. "Physicians don't usually guess at such a thing, Miss Keeley. If you would care to tell me, I'm sure that would be a helpful start."

"I am forty-six."

Most physicians would be as successful as Scarlet was now in not showing his amazement. And then, of course, there was his theatrical training. She went on before he could say anything.

"Up until two months ago, doctor, I simply felt my age, and I think I looked it. But that began to change, with alarming rapidity. And now, you see the old woman across from you." She sighed deeply. "I am afraid that if you were to wait another few months, I won't be around for you to ask me any questions. So please, ask me now, and let me know whether we can get to the bottom of this horrible change that is happening to me."

For all of the absurdity of the woman's adherence to youthful fashion, it was a sober and unflinching request, and Scarlet was moved by it.

"Have your habits changed in any way?"

"No."

"Your regularity? I mean—"

"I know what you mean. No."

"Have you experienced pain anywhere? Difficulty breathing? A change in your normal sleep patterns?"

"None."

"Have you altered your diet?"

"I have not. I eat sparingly, and I believe, healthily."

"Has there been any change in your environment? Do you have new wallpaper or carpeting? Any new plants introduced into your home?"

"Are you serious?"

"Yes, I am."

"Then the answer once again is no."

And now the age-old response of physicians throughout history.

"Let's have a look."

The physical examination, while revealing nothing unusual, was paradoxical. The heart, lungs, pulse, blood flow in the carotid and the pedal pulse in the feet, and reflexes were all normal. The pupil response and appearance of the eyes was unremarkable, except for a well-developed age-related cataract in the right eye. The ears and mouth were without infection; and palpitation of the stomach showed no pain or tenderness. The patient was in relatively good shape for a woman in her mid- to late-seventies.

Further questions elicited no new information concerning anything that had changed in her life over the past two months. There was nothing, except an unexplained—what doctors call an 'idiopathic'—increase in how rapidly this woman was aging.

Scarlet didn't even know if this was a disease, syndrome, or condition; the terms were slippery at best. He would consult his medical books later today, once his morning surgery hours were over. In the meantime, he had nothing to offer the former Mrs. Walter Keeley-Campbell, who now preferred to once again be called Miss Harriet Keeley.

In terms of social affairs and invitations to balls and dinners, she might, for all he knew, be reverting to her youth. But her body appeared to be hurtling headlong in the opposite direction.

CHAPTER 5

The Master of Illusion

 ork, as always, was a voracious monster that greedily ate most of his time that spring. An employed physician in Victoria's England was someone who didn't have to worry about the economic upheavals and downturns of the age, such as the Panic of 1857, or the recession of 1867-1869 (both originating in that new powerhouse of the global economy, America). Of course, the police surgeon also enjoyed secure employment from a phenomenon that was never in danger of waning: crime, and the impact on medicine which it produced. And so Scarlet's days were as busy as ever.

He was unsuccessful in diagnosing the disease or condition afflicting Mrs. Keeley-Campbell ("Miss Keeley"). His Hoblyn[*] had nothing to say on it; indeed, the book apparently didn't consider "aging" to be a term requiring definition! There were also no monographs or scientific papers on the subject. He was reduced to sending a note to his patient, advocating plenty of rest and daily walks in the fresh air. He told her he would like to see her again in a month, and left it at that.

A Wednesday afternoon brought a note on the personal

---

[*] Richard D. Hoblyn, M.A., *A Dictionary of Terms Used in Medicine and the Collateral Sciences*, 11th ed. (1887) was the standard medical dictionary of the period.

stationery of Django Pierce-Jones, informing him that his friend had procured two tickets to Max von Leiden's *Phantasmagoria* at the Queen Victoria Theatre Royal for that Friday evening. The note ended with a threat of the dire consequences to follow if Scarlet turned down the opportunity to see this "damned difficult to get tickets for" show.

Scarlet had forgotten the magicians' rivalry, his own fleeting interest in magic, and Marco the Magnificent's *The Cabalistic Laboratory* show. But the chance to see Marco's great rival, the German conjurer Max von Leiden, seemed just the thing to alleviate the exacting and mundane routine of his duties as a police surgeon.

Scarlet was expecting a performance which was similar to Marco's show which he had seen with Catherine Wilson. But he was completely surprised.

He shouldn't have been. On the ride to the theatre, Django had informed him of the differences between Messrs. Caliosto ("Marco") and von Leiden.

"The German's show is much darker," Django had said. "You'll notice immediately, for instance, how the lighting is more somber, as this magician uses darkness and shadows to great effect. They must do something different with the footlights as well, because somehow von Leiden always looks like he's being lit from below, with the eerie result that has. But the best effect is the magician himself."

"How so?"

"He absolutely looks the part of a mesmerist. He's extremely tall—well over the six-foot mark—and painfully thin, to the point where one wonders if the fellow eats at all. He has jet-black hair, obviously dyed, and bushy black eyebrows which meet above his nose as if he's perpetually frowning. He also sports very long black moustaches which meet in a pointed goatee."

"I see. A dark character, indeed, at least in his stage persona. Anything else?"

"Yes—a mesmerist's eyes. Very large, with the whites showing around big pupils, as though they are staring right through you."

"Sounds more like Graves's Disease or hyperthyroidism," countered Scarlet. "But that's the second time you mentioned mesmerism. Is that part of his act?"

"Oh, yes. He's very much the dark wizard, ensnaring his victims. Well, willing victims, since they're audience volunteers."

"Why? Does he cause them harm in any way?"

"No, no," replied Django. "It's all in the spirit of harmless magical entertainment. Except—" and he hesitated.

"Except what?"

"Well, he's been known to rather humiliate people on stage, just a bit, from time to time."

"Charming," said Scarlet.

"It's part of his persona," added Pierce-Jones. "Though, if I were to guess, I'd say the behavior is due as much to the man as the stage character. And it undoubtedly adds to his attraction. One never knows, you see, when he will decide to display that side of himself."

"Still, I would think something like that would make people uncomfortable and not want to attend his shows."

Django laughed. "Apparently, that's not our theatre-going public," he said. "And that, by the way, is one of the principal interests in the *Phantasmagoria* show: what *might* happen. It's one of the reasons people flock to his shows."

"How so?"

"Herr von Leiden has a trick—what he calls a 'philosophical experiment'—that is well advertised, but seldom performed."

Django made a sign to stop Scarlet's intended interruption.

"It's called 'Your Fondest Wish.' And it's something to boggle the mind. A volunteer from the audience is mesmerized, and made to reveal the thing they most desire. While this is happening, behind the magician and the volunteer we begin to see scenes connected with this person's wish being acted out. And at the end, von Leiden tells the person that henceforth their wish shall be granted."

"It's obviously a plant," Scarlet protested. "The magician could never put together scenes from the person's life—supposedly—without knowing beforehand what it was going to show. It's a theatrical impossibility."

"Not for 'The Master of Illusion,' people say. And then there are the rumors that the volunteers' lives *were* changed from then on, according to their fondest wish."

"Don't be absurd!" said Scarlet.

"Nevertheless, that is the word on the street about von Leiden." He raised his eyebrows. "You can see why it's nearly impossible to get a ticket to the show. Everyone is hoping that the trick will be performed that night. And that they will be the one chosen."

A long line of black hansoms was queued up on Haymarket in front of the Queen Victoria Theatre Royal, indistinguishable except for the various colors the cab owners had painted on the spokes or rims of the oversized wheels. Pierce-Jones rapped on the trap with his walking stick and then paid the cabman, since they'd have to walk to the theatre entrance from here.

Whatever the relative merits of Marco's and von Leiden's shows, for Scarlet the experience of attending the respective theatres was intriguing in itself. Covent Garden, where he and Catherine Wilson had seen Marco's show, was vast. It held three sets of stalls downstairs—the largest in the center and one on each side of the two aisles—and three balconies, all of it encompassing a staggering 3,800 seats.

The Queen Victoria Theatre Royal, which they entered now, seemed modest by comparison. Its design featured a single set of stalls with no center aisle; a Royal Circle; upper circle; and small gallery, with a combined seating capacity of 894 patrons. Covent Garden had plush seats of crimson and gold-painted balconies; the Queen Victoria, dark-blue seats with golden galleries *and* walls.

Scarlet sensed that von Leiden had deliberately chosen the smaller venue over the vast emporium. Here, things were much more intimate. The flames in the gas lights, for instance, usually at full brightness while the audience members searched for their seats, were turned down low. The subdued lighting and dark-blue seats also made the atmosphere more mysterious. The front curtain, lowered now, was also blue, a half-shade lighter in color than the seat cushions. From the apron which jutted forward of the curtain, they could see that the stage floor was painted black.

The location of their tickets was decidedly better than Scarlet and Catherine's had been for Caliosto's *The Cabalistic Laboratory* show at Covent Garden. He and Pierce-Jones occupied seats P17 and P18 of the main stalls, which were on the aisle at stage-left. He reasoned that fourteen rows from the stage in the stalls must be a capital location to watch a first-class magic show.

When the curtain rose, however, he was disappointed. There was nothing on stage but a small wooden table with two large glass decanters on it, one filled with water and the other with a deep-red liquid. No cabinets sat on stage for the magician or his assistant to step in and out of—nor anything else, for that matter. A bare space with that small table and a stage painted black was all there was. You could even see the brick wall at the back of the stage and theatrical rigging everywhere.

So far, *Phantasmagoria* offered no setting like the vaguely medieval Arabia of Marco the Magnificent's show. To Scarlet, the strategy seemed either foolhardy or indicative of massive confidence.

After a long two or three minutes of the empty stage, von Leiden appeared, striding from the wings to take his place behind the simple table. He was dressed in the standard magician's outfit: black tails with a severe cutaway in front but with more room at the sides, a white waistcoat, and an oversized black bow tie. But there was no carnation in the buttonhole or white handkerchief in the breast pocket to alleviate the severity of the costume. As to the man himself: the severe features, jet-black hair, and piercing eyes were exactly as Pierce-Jones had described them, even when viewed from fourteen rows back.

Max von Leiden stood with perfect physical stillness and poise. Now raising his right arm, he prepared to address his audience, the face completely expressionless. When he spoke, the voice—in complete contrast to Caliosto's—was deep and resonant, compelling everyone's attention immediately. It filled the intimate Queen Victoria theatre with ease.

"Welcome to *Phantasmagoria*—where nothing is as it seems! . . . Like life itself, yes?"

There was no "Ladies and gentlemen, welcome to our show!" or other standard banter. Somehow, the atmosphere already seemed at a high pitch, though nothing had happened yet.

Stepping aside so that the right arm now indicated the table with its two filled decanters, von Leiden declared:

"We will begin with a miracle! Can you ask for more? See the two Karaffen . . . excuse me, carafes. One contains water, the other wine. It would be impossible to turn one into the other, would it not? We have heard that this was done once, but who knows? Tonight, however, you will *see* this miracle accomplished before your very eyes!"

At this point, Django leaned over and whispered into his friend's ear: "Standard magic practice. Whatever trick is coming up, it should be preceded by banter or stage business alerting the audience that something extraordinary is about to happen."

Listening to Django, Scarlet missed what the magician had just said, but saw that he now held a large, printed scarf in front of him at waist-level. He positioned himself behind the table once again, draping the scarf over the front of it. After a long flourish in which the scarf was made to turn inside and out, he whipped the scarf up over his head. There on the table were the two decanters in the same positions, except now the liquids inside them had been reversed.

"As you see," said von Leiden in his booming voice, "I have turned the wine into water—unlike the first time this experiment was attempted, during which the opposite occurred, making everyone drunk!"

The applause began slightly late, though it was strong enough. Scarlet wondered if it would have been quicker and even stronger without Herr von Leiden's blasphemous joke.

"You will find, my friends," the magician continued, "that the show you witness tonight is unique." A female assistant in a vivid red robe was now removing the table and decanters, proving that von Leiden wasn't above using the standard element of attractive helpers in his act.

"Other magicians claim that their sleight of hand and devices only appear to defy natural laws. My power *does* defy those laws. They may keep their Hocus Pocus! They conjure to give the appearance of reality. I give you my experiments—which are real, and only have the appearance of trickery!

"Tonight, you will experience true mesmerism, as we delve into the dark place between reality and illusion. Prepare for the wonderful and mysterious! And now, my friends—*Phantasmagoria!*"

And for the next two hours, the noble art of trickery—or as von Leiden would have it, dark experiments which defied the laws of nature—was on display. The show was dazzling, in both the 'experiments' themselves and the pace at which they succeeded one another.

Stage business was taken care of by two female assistants clothed not in garish costumes, but in those scarlet robes that looked vaguely religious in nature. The overall effect was of a high priest from some ancient time conjuring in service to a deity. This priest was dark, however; and so, presumably, must be the deity.

During the series of illusions which followed, it came home to Scarlet that any great magician isn't really a trickster at all, but a consummate actor playing the part of a magician. Herr von Leiden played the parts openly, announcing his persona as it changed from time to time. "Call me Pendragon!" he would say as he explained what the audience was about to see. Then, "Now I am the Mikado's conjurer" as he performed a different illusion. "Do you recognize Eunus of Sicily?" And: "I was Merlin when I accomplished this dazzling feat for the first time."

He drew a magic circle on stage, employing angled mirrors so the audience could see it. *Six* volunteers were invited to step inside it—a number that was unheard of in terms of participants from the audience. Once they were within the circle, von Leiden summoned an electrical storm that lit up the entire stage with lightning bolts. But each one evaporated at the edge of the circle, leaving the people inside unharmed.

In a completely baffling demonstration, he announced that he was now Circe, the enchantress of the mythical island of Aeaea in Homer's *Odyssey*—and turned five male volunteers *into swine* (or at least, men with swines' heads) and back again, in full view of the audience!

"Welcome to my world!" he proclaimed at one point, his voice a booming presence of its own. "My countryman, Goethe, once said, 'The highest problem of any art is to cause, by appearance, the illusion of a higher reality.' Surely you are aware by now that my art exceeds such a description—for *I give you the true reality you have been unaware of until now.*"

He wrung the head off a goose and restored it again immediately. He wore what seemed a cruel smile as he did this, as if to say to the crowd: "Indeed, what is your reality if mine can take and restore life at will?"

A female audience member was invited onstage—"You, madam, are, I believe, the lady we are looking for"—and told that she was an adulterous wife known for her trysts in her part of London (which remained unnamed). "But do not fear, everyone . . . divine justice is coming!" The magician then produced a wax crocodile "seven inches long, ladies and gentlemen," holding it aloft so that all could see. He bent down and set it on stage, where it instantly became *seven feet* long, and devoured the poor woman, who disappeared, and only seconds later reappeared in the aisle next to her row of seats.

To Scarlet, the show was disorienting and scandalous and even blasphemous where the magician's claims of defying reality were concerned. But it was undeniably dazzling, even breathtaking, to a degree which seemed remarkable for a sophisticated London audience.

There was also a question in his mind that he believed must be forming in the audience's minds as well: Who is this person who can seemingly play with reality in this way, and even boast about it?

"At this time," von Leiden was saying, "I will employ the magic of the priest-magicians of ancient Mesopotamia—the 'magi'—whom I knew well. I will perform the forbidden act known as 'The Rising.'"

The gas jets dimmed further in both the house and on stage. Von Leiden waited, then said:

"I must ask for your complete silence. For now, I will perform the delicate and Herculean task of raising the dead. I will summon Ninlil herself—the Mesopotamian Goddess of Declaring Destinies!"

The entire theatre, and all eight hundred and ninety-four souls within it, was now as silent as a tomb.

Von Leiden stood stock still, his head bowed low. Slowly, his arms rose until they were held out from his body with the palms facing the stage floor. His voice rose to a level of extraordinary power:

"RISE, NINLIL, WIFE OF ENLIL! I COMMAND YOU TO RISE! . . . RISE, AS YOU ROSE IN YOUR TEMPLE IN THE CITY OF MARI ON THE GREAT EUPHRATES RIVER, FOUR THOUSAND YEARS AGO!"

Where his gaze appeared to penetrate the stage floor, something was happening.

A small cloud of blue haze appeared—not quite smoke, more like mist. The mist became a column, then began to take on a vaguely human shape. Within a minute or two, no more, the shape became a woman—head, shoulders, arms, and torso—but whose lower half remained only a column of the blue mist, tapering to an unseen source in the stage floor.

The woman's bronze-colored hair was free-flowing at the sides and back but braided on each side in front. She was dressed in green and gold: a gold band on her forehead; leaf-shaped large earrings of the same color; and an elaborate golden necklace resting on a green dress that was open at the belly but wrapped around her hips tightly. The summoned figure hovered, swaying back and forth slightly in the air currents: substantial but not solid, as though its journey from wherever it had come from was not quite complete.

The magician stood downstage of the floating vision and to the side, so as not to block anyone's view. He made a small, courteous bow, then spoke to it.

"Who are you?"

"I am Ninlil, goddess of my people," said the wraith, in a haughty female voice. "Who has summoned me in this way? Be quick in your answer, or you shall wear the collar of a dog, and if you displease me more, be thrown into the fire!"

But Herr von Leiden laughed.

"You have no power here," he said. "And certainly none over me. I am The Master of Illusion, and I have summoned you here to demonstrate my prowess."

There was a long pause, and then the woman in the vision spoke again. Her voice now was more even—one might say more careful.

"What is it you wish?"

"Merely to speak with you," the magician answered lightly. "You are the goddess of Declaring Destinies, are you not?"

"I am. There is no other who possesses my power."

"Excellent! Then let us observe your magnificent ability." Von Leiden turned toward the audience. "Who would like to ask the goddess something? Whose destiny does one of you wish to learn about?"

A loud female voice came from the second balcony:

"When will me old man stop drinkin' and bring home some money for a change?"

Laughter throughout the house. Von Leiden smiled and held up his hands, palms outward.

"Please! May I have a serious question?"

A gentleman in evening dress stood up three rows behind Scarlet and Pierce-Jones, at the center of the downstairs stalls. He cleared his throat, and asked in a loud voice:

"What does the next decade hold for British foreign policy?"

There was immediate silence—what Scarlet thought of as a shocked silence. Von Leiden nodded as if to express his gratitude for the question, then turned to the vision, still wavering at center-stage. Surely, thought Scarlet and Pierce-Jones both, the magician had painted himself into a corner.

But Ninlil spoke.

"There will be a period of disappointments for your people," she proclaimed. "For the ten years you ask about, and a bit longer, your empire will become increasingly isolated. You will suffer military misadventures and the destruction of alliances, and ultimately will find yourself standing alone."

Von Leiden turned back to the audience with a "There you are" look on his face, as a collective outcry immediately rent the air. As if with one voice, cries of dismay and outrage resounded, and many in the crowd stood to point their fingers at the stage or shake their fists. But the magician remained calm, facing this wall of sound with a confident and even satisfied look on his face.

When it had subsided enough for him to be heard, he raised his voice, projecting the sound so that the entire interior of the theatre would hear him easily:

"Have you heard enough?"

At the unanimous positive acclamation, he raised his right hand high. Now he bent from the waist, and gathering momentum, swept his hand through the air and hurled the spell toward the "goddess," commanding:

"BEGONE!"

And at once the swirl of mist contracted and disappeared, as if sucked into the floor itself.

Both arms in the air now, and a deep bow. And as The Master of Illusion straightened again:

"Ladies and gentlemen—goodnight!"

CHAPTER 6

A Lamentable Tour de Force

urtains rose at 8.30 p.m. in the West End for plays and magic shows alike so that theatregoers could have a dinner hour. But there were always restaurants to be found open after the closing curtains in the densely-packed theatre district. Scarlet and Pierce-Jones were enjoying a late meal at Rouget's on Castle Street in Leicester Square. The restaurant was only a half-mile from where they had just seen *Phantasmagoria* at the Queen Victoria Theatre Royal in Haymarket.

Over sole l'anglaise for Scarlet and striped bass Brettone for Pierce-Jones, the two discussed the show they had just seen.

Django started the conversation with one word, once the waiter had gathered the menus again and head toward the kitchen.

"Amazing."

"And disturbing," Scarlet countered immediately.

"An extraordinary artist, though."

"Yes, there is no doubting that," said his physician friend. "His illusions are quite inexplicable."

Django laughed. "It wouldn't be much of a magic show if you guessed how he did any of it, would it?"

Scarlet conceded the point with a slight nod.

"It's not the magic that disturbed me," he added.

Now Django nodded. "You mean von Leiden."

"Yes," said Scarlet. "And I would use the word deplorable."

"Aren't you confusing the artist and his art?"

"What do you mean?"

"You should know that magicians consider the mechanics of magic, and even their manipulative skills in using it, to be rubbish. It's the intellectual pursuit that they regard as art."

"I can understand that," replied Scarlet. "And using those standards, von Leiden must rule the roost. I'll admit that the art displayed on that stage tonight was of a very high order. All the same, I can't help but think that there is another effect von Leiden is aiming for. Not merely stage magic, I mean. He seems to be saying other, larger things."

Their wine came, and Django waited until it was poured and the sommelier had left.

"Such as what?" he asked.

"Well, this business about reality. He claims that he isn't trying to give the illusion of a higher reality, but to make all of us aware of the true reality we've been ignoring . . . or something along those lines. That's an extraordinary thing for a magician to say."

"'Yes, well—"

"Don't you find it disturbing?"

"I suppose I do," Django answered. "I wouldn't have used that word—but yes, I think you're right."

"There's something else. A magician is supposed to be good-natured and benign, someone who charms and woos his audience."

"And Herr von Leiden is intentionally the opposite."

"I should say so!" replied Scarlet." He set his wine glass down and leaned forward. "It's almost as if he disdains the tradition. The whole show, and the man himself, are really . . . I don't know, like creations of darkness rather than light. Those black looks, the commanding voice, the piercing eyes . . . the whole thing is mesmeric in terms of how he controls his audience."

"As though he were in another class from ordinary magicians?" Django offered.

"Exactly," replied Scarlet. "He even says it near the beginning of the show, something like: '*I don't perform parlour magic. My power is far greater. I give you the true reality!*'"

"So, he's simply a monomaniac?"

"I'm not sure," countered Scarlet. "But there seems to be something else there. Something much deeper."

The two were well into their meals when Pierce-Jones made his own observation.

"During the performance, I was thinking along the lines you were talking about a few minutes ago. I thought that something seemed odd or out of place, but I couldn't put my finger on it. But your label of 'disturbing' fits it well, I think." He considered how to explain what he was thinking so that Scarlet would understand him. "Magicians are supposed to misdirect audiences and weaken their powers of observation, aren't they?"

"Yes, naturally."

"Von Leiden was doing something different though, wasn't he? I mean, it seemed to me that he was trying to get people to think and feel differently." He considered what he'd said and decided it was the idea he'd wanted to express. "What kind of magician does that?"

Scarlet didn't need to find an answer. He'd already expressed it earlier.

"The disturbing kind," he said.

CHAPTER 7

Post-Mortem of an Old Girl

he following week brought Scarlet a curious case for autopsy. It was another instance of an unsuspicious death, but one which the post-mortem facilities at the local hospitals were simply too backed-up to deal with. That was the only reason he ended up with a case that took him on a wild emotional ride consisting of confusion, shock, and horror.

The decedent was listed in the 1889 Post Mortem and Case Book as "Charlotte Tibbins, 16, school girl." But after he had checked on the autopsy tools already set out in the dissecting room in the basement of the Yard and removed the sheet from the body, he saw immediately that there had been a mistake. This was quite obviously the body of an elderly woman. He checked the toe tag. It read:

Tibbins, Charlotte, 23 Apr 1889

The error irked him, of course, but nothing more. He replaced the sheet and walked down the hall to find the mortuary assistant. On this shift that was Samuel Groat, who'd been with the Yard for many years. Groat insisted that he had prepared and washed the correct cadaver for the scheduled procedure.

Scarlet returned to the dissecting room, took off the sheet once more, and looked more carefully at the body before him. What in the world was going on? He was looking at an elderly female whose death, he would guess, was at least in part caused by old age. He would know more when he went inside, of course. But this manifestly wasn't the body of a schoolgirl. Could it be someone's ghastly joke? The thought was so grotesque that he dismissed it from his mind immediately.

Whatever the casebook said in terms of a right or wrong entry, he was the medical examiner scheduled to perform this autopsy. The chief coroner's office had the responsibility to correct the error, not him. Holding a scalpel now, Scarlet examined the body on the dissecting table more closely.

The deceased exhibited all the external signs of a sufficiently-nourished female who had simply reached the end of her life span. It was true that a pronounced cyanosis or bluish tint was present in the lips, fingertips, and fingernails. But this result of low blood oxygen was usually caused by heart disease or some form of obstruction in the lungs; and again, was most commonly found among the elderly. He was sure he would find the signs of one or both of those etiologies upon internal examination.

Otherwise, Charlotte Tibbins—or whoever she was—showed all of the ordinary effects of aging. The body was fair of complexion and the woman had probably once been blonde, though the hair was now completely white and much thinned. The skin was loosened everywhere, most noticeably at the neck where it was crisscrossed with deep hatch-lines, and at the elbows and knees. Fine lines and wrinkles were present everywhere on the face, especially in the high malar area under the eyes, where the fat pads once present were gone. Deeper wrinkles marked the nasolabial folds between the nose and mouth. The eyebrows were mostly drawn by pencil, as hair was absent where it had once been present. The lips were almost vanishingly thin. There was also marked periorbital hyperpigmentation, or excessively dark circles under the eyes. This was mildly surprising in a fair-complected person, since such darkening was characteristic of skin that contained a high level of melanin.

The sclera—the white part of the eye—was yellow, indicating jaundice. The skin was heavily spotted on the hands and the temples. The overall appearance of the face was gaunt, with pronounced loss of tissue between the zygoma or bony arch of the cheek, and the mandible, so that the cheeks "caved in" noticeably. The breasts sagged with the typical appearance they took on from decades of the effects of gravity.

Following a Y-shaped incision in the chest and abdomen down to the pubis, Scarlet went in. The most significant initial finding was that the deceased suffered from severe coronary artery disease, with a clear indication of atherosclerosis. Stenosis was observed in the aortic value opening, with scarring present that would have restricted blood flow from the left ventricle to the aorta. He did not, however, see any evidence of a coronary thrombosis or pulmonary embolism.

As soon as Scarlet saw the liver, he decided that the decedent probably suffered from hepatitis. It was brownish in appearance, rather than the red-brown of a healthy organ, though without the obvious gross changes that came with cirrhosis or fatty liver disease. This appearance, along with the jaundice he'd noted, indicated hepatitis, which makes the liver less able to rid itself of the red-orange compound bilirubin through its bile ducts, resulting in yellow-appearing skin. In addition, the notes on this patient from when she had presented at hospital were also consistent with end-stage liver failure: confusion and disorientation, lethargy and fatigue, poor appetite, nausea, and an overall marked decrease in alertness.

Two hours and ten minutes after he began, Scarlet completed the post-mortem examination and sewed up the autopsy incision. He would list the COD as acute liver failure compounded by sclerotic artery disease, with an additional finding of jaundice. And—though he wouldn't be able to write it in the case book—old age.

What he *could* do was head up to Mallinson's office, regarding what he thought was a major cock-up in Scotland Yard's Medical Department. He had no intention of singling out any of the mortuary assistants for negligence. But the Yard simply couldn't accept such grossly sloppy recordkeeping.

He found the chief surgeon in his natural habitat and state: at his desk, writing out some memorandum or official bulletin behind stacks of paperwork and looking all the more miserable because of it. Sir Edward Mallinson's liver had never had a problem releasing sufficient bile, and then some.

The scratching of the pen stopped, though Mallinson didn't change a thing in terms of his posture or attitude except the direction of his gaze.

"Scarlet. What is it?"

"I beg your pardon for the interruption, sir. I'm afraid there's been a mistake in identifying a patient for autopsy. I just finished—"

"Please don't tell me you've dissected someone who was still alive."

With the right tone of voice or timing—or especially, with another personality behind it—the attempt at autopsy humor might have worked. Scarlet managed a slight, tight upturning of his lips at the corners. He shook his head.

"It's a misidentification. Rather an egregious one, I'm afraid."

That prompted a setting down of the pen, a straightening of the posture, and the intertwining of the fingers of one hand with that of the other.

"Shit. Have a seat, William." And when Scarlet had accepted the offer: "Tell me about it."

Both the 'William,' and the opportunity for an actual conversation showed that, despite the mountain of paperwork on the desk, Mallinson was in an approachable mood. Miracles apparently did still exist.

"I was scheduled for a PM on a 'Charlotte Tibbins,' age 16,"

Scarlet began. "Instead, the prepared body was an elderly woman, I'd say in her mid-eighties at least. I have no idea what her name is. I just finished. Apparently, someone else must be scheduled for that woman's autopsy, and will find themselves with a school girl on the table instead."

"Extraordinary. And the cause of death?"

"Take your pick," Scarlet responded. "Some doctors still use 'old age,' don't they? Officially, hepatic liver disease, including jaundice, with coronary artery disease as a contributing factor."

Dr. Mallinson made a dismissive sound and shook his head. Then he repeated himself: "That's extraordinary. Nothing else? What about Hutchinson's Syndrome?[*] Was there ectodermal dysplasia?"

"No," Scarlet answered. "And the thought had occurred to me. But there were no characteristic signs in the hair, teeth, or nails that indicated dysplasia. And the atrophy I saw seemed clearly age-related—nothing like what Hutchinson described in that three-year-old boy. He said the boy had an 'old-man appearance.' The woman I just autopsied was not a young girl who appeared old. She was an elderly woman who died of liver and heart-related conditions typical for her age."

"So you believe this was nothing more than a mix-up in terms of the records and autopsy assignments?"

"Obviously," replied Scarlet, trying not to make the word sound sarcastic.

"I see," said Dr. Mallinson, and stood. "Thank you, Dr. Scarlet. I appreciate your letting me know right away. I will look into it

---

[*] In 1886, English physician Jonathan Hutchinson had described a three-and-a-half year old boy who had the appearance of an old man. Another Englishman, surgeon Hastings Gilford, would describe a similar syndrome in 1897. The disease then acquired the name Hutchinson-Gilford progeria syndrome, the genetic disease which is now known as progeria, in which children age prematurely and typically die by the age of 15.

immediately."

And Mallinson did. That afternoon, Scarlet received a handwritten note from his superior while he was at his own desk in his office at the Yard and dealing with his own piles of paperwork.

The chief surgeon informed him that no error had occurred. The body he autopsied was that of a 16-year-old school girl named Charlotte Tibbins.

The oil lamp on Scarlet's desk had gone empty, and he was sitting in the semi-darkness nearly an hour later, when a colleague poked his head in and asked if he would like company walking outside to hail a cab.

CHAPTER 8

Fame and Cruelty

ondon's magic war went on, to the great satisfaction of two theatrical landlords and the magicians who had rented their venues. Giuseppe Caliosto, Marco the Magnificent, continued to fill vast Covent Garden. A half-mile away, Max von Leiden, The Master of Illusion, alternately outraged and thrilled patrons at the Queen Victoria Theatre Royal.

By the end of April, von Leiden had three weeks remaining in his eight-week run. Caliosto, who had booked a twelve-week season, held a two-week option to continue his show until the middle of June if ticket sales remained strong. So far, they did.

Yet nothing was as volatile as the Season[*] when it came to headlines and lurid gossip, and so it proved once again this spring.

For a time at least, the magic craze gave way to the latest scandal of the most famous libertine in England, Oliver Wyatt.

And what a delicious scandal it was!

Twenty-four-year-old Oliver was the second son of Thomas Wyatt, the 10th Viscount Huddersfield, who owned lands in Lancaster and Yorkshire. In fact, the Wyatts were said to have had

---

[*] Editor's Note: The annual period from April – September when the elite of British society showed themselves in a social whirl of balls, dinner parties, flower shows, horse-racing, and cricket matches. It was also the time when debutants were formally introduced into society.

ancestors on both sides of the mid-fifteenth-century Wars of the Roses—some of whom had pledged allegiance to the red rose of Lancaster, and some to the white rose of York.

A city dweller rather than an occupant of his father's rural estate, Oliver nevertheless seemed to consider it his full-time occupation to sow as many wild oats as possible. He was a peacock who was as often in the news for his wit as for his lifestyle. Both provided a plentiful supply of fodder for the voracious British press.

He had attended Cambridge, where he read biology as preparation for a medical degree. But at just 60 miles away, the gambling dens of Soho and Piccadilly were just too close to St. Edmunds College where Oliver was enrolled. He had left Cambridge in his junior year, dedicating himself to the life of a dissolute young aristocrat. From then on, friends and debtors could find him without fail at White's, at Brook's, or at The Turf Club, idling the night away with fellow libertines at whist and hazard.

Wyatt didn't shy away from scandal; he lived for it. He'd even remarked on it once, if the rumour about him was to be believed. When confronted by a Church of England prelate about his immoral behavior, he had supposedly turned to the priest and said: "Great Heaven! But why not, dear man? Carrying out crimes only lands you in jail—but if you're determined on damnation, committing sins is your first-class ticket!"

He seemed to smoke and quip with equal abandon. When seen carrying a lamp in some drawing room or other and asked jokingly if he was seeking an honest man, he replied, "Goodness, no, old fellow. I'm simply looking for a light." Asked at another time if he thought he was going to heaven, he answered: "I'm quite sure of it. You will certainly find me in a cloud . . . of smoke. Kindly tell my tobacconist where to find me, won't you? I can only afford the brand of cigarettes he sells when I'm either in debt or dead—which are very much the same thing, of course."

Young Wyatt's antics and *bons mots* were ambrosia for an elite London society ravenous for both. Even Lord Salisbury—in his second stint as Prime Minister—found time to comment on the ongoing scandal in some of his private letters.

And yet Oliver Wyatt seemed determined to race ahead of everyone's attempts to keep up with his private life. His sexual escapades were legendary, even for someone so young. It was well known that Oliver didn't care if his lovers wore skirts or trousers, and in fact his most notorious affairs were with the sons of other aristocratic fathers like his own. There were constant rumours that one of those families would bring morals charges against him in court, though it hadn't happened yet.

On the Friday before the last weekend in April—when there would be plenty of time for everyone to gossip about it—Oliver had been caught up in the net when the police raided a molly house[*] in Moorgate in East London. The fourteen men who were detained were brought before the magistrate the next day—eight of them still wearing the women's clothing they had been arrested in the previous evening—where the entire group was charged with "all manner of gross and vile obscenity."

In Wyatt's case, when asked under oath if he had said he would "go forty miles to enjoy" one of the other men present (as that man had bragged in his own testimony), Oliver denied it. "My feet are rather too flat, your honour," he had replied. "I might have said I'd go around the corner to be with him, but not an inch more."

The reply brought a laugh to more than one listener and reader. But for once, it seemed that Oliver Wyatt had strayed too far beyond the norms of behavior and decency to escape with impunity. Sentencing would follow sometime early in the next week. In the meantime, the young man was said to be in hiding somewhere in London where, for once, he apparently was not interested in being seen or heard.

In the end, the sentencing was inconsequential (whether or not

---

[*] A molly house was a meeting place for men to socialize or meet sexual partners, and where some men cross-dressed as women.

due to the Viscount Huddersfield's influence), and the rumour mill went on to other things. What one wag called "The Trials and Titillations of Oliver Wyatt" would have to wait until another day to add a new chapter to the deliciously salacious and never ending scandal.

SCARLET DID FURTHER RESEARCH on 16-year-old Charlotte Tibbins's inexplicable death, but he was unsuccessful in learning anything new. The closest description he could find in the medical literature was Dr. Jonathan Hutchinson's experience three years ago with the 3 ½-year-old boy who had the appearance of an old man. But the girl in the autopsy Scarlet conducted didn't appear old— she *was* old; and her organs and the rest of her physiology displayed the changes characteristic of extreme age.

He resigned himself to the possibility that this death was simply an anomaly. On the other hand, he would certainly write his own paper on his findings for the benefit of other physicians who might find themselves facing a similar mystifying case. It was the way of science. Little by little, and doctor by doctor, his profession accumulated enough evidence that a once-unfathomable condition would become well understood—or if it was too rare for that to happen—at least recognized.

HE READ IN ONE of the papers that the run of Max von Leiden's magic show had been extended a second time until the middle of June, meaning that, coincidentally, he and Caliosto would end their runs at about the same time. He'd also heard that the German magician had incorporated into his act a young female audience volunteer who, it turned out, was an amateur magician herself. Von Leiden was allowing her to perform some tricks (undoubtedly with his tutelage) on stage. Scarlet tried to imagine the dark magician as a benign father figure giving the girl a chance to enter the profession, and couldn't.

From time to time, he would hear of the famous and rarely performed segment of *Phantasmagoria* called "Your Fondest Wish" that Pierce-Jones had mentioned at their dinner at the Athenaeum Club. This was the moment when Max von Leiden would choose someone from the audience to come on stage and be mesmerized. The magician would then question the person about their life and receive—supposedly—truthful answers due to the mesmeric influence.

Then, at some point, he would tell the person to share with him and the audience what they wanted more than anything in life: their "fondest wish." Scarlet wasn't quite sure from the bits and pieces he'd picked up what happened next. But apparently, scenes from the person's life played out behind where the volunteer and von Leiden stood on stage. Brought out of the mesmeric trance by the magician at the end of the act, the volunteer was told that their fondest wish was granted.

"Your Fondest Wish" made such audacious—indeed, one could say they were miraculous—claims that it caused people to purchase tickets to *Phantasmagoria* in droves, in spite of any belief they may have had that it must all be a hoax. And, naturally, there *were* rumours of people's lives that had been turned around because their fondest wish had come true. After all, the theatre had always been a place that projected society's dreams, as well as mirroring its fears and anxieties.

It was all rubbish as far as Scarlet was concerned—a triumph of conjurers and promoters, nothing more.

Yet when Django announced that he'd bought tickets for another showing of *Phantasmagoria*, Scarlet wasn't too hard on himself for accepting the invitation. After all, he thought, 'There are more things in heaven and earth, Horatio, than are dreamt of in your philosophy.'

Which was another way of telling himself, "You're a hypocrite, Will Scarlet. Enjoy the show."

BUT OTHER EVENTS WERE to occur first in this, London's magical year. Two deaths—both related to magic shows—swept society up in a wave of excitement, morbid curiosity, and rampant speculation.

The first was the shocking death on stage of Giuseppe Caliosto, Marco the Magnificent himself. Tragically (or sensationally, if your mind worked that way), his death came during the illusion well recognized for its high level of risk: the Bullet Catch.

Marco wasn't the first magician to die this way. In Dublin in 1818, a performer known as Kia Khan Kruse was killed during the Bullet Catch—shot to death by the volunteer's gun, which the man had drawn and used before anyone could stop him. Two years later, a Polish magician placed his wife-assistant in front of six actual bodyguards of a prince of the region, and she was killed when one of the guards "misunderstood the instructions." Also in 1820, a conjurer named Scott lost part of his face "when a fun-loving spectator dropped a button into the gun he was loading." And exactly twenty years ago in Paris in 1869, a magician known as Dr. Epstein rammed the bullet into the gun with his magic wand, left a piece of the wand in the barrel (which had broken without him realizing it), and was killed on stage when the wooden projectile was fired from the weapon.[*]

Caliosto's death was not explainable in any of these ways, however. First, the volunteer who was brought on stage to inspect and hand the bullets to the captain of the firing squad was a woman—and she was not seen to produce a handgun from the folds of her skirt and discharge it at the magician. The rifles were fired by the six "Ottoman" soldiers, just as they had been in the show that Scarlet and Pierce-Jones attended, with the identical procedures followed as they were every night.

Inexplicably, however, on that night Marco had taken two very

---

[*] Editor's note: These real-life examples are taken from magician James Randi's marvelous history of magic, *Conjuring* (New York: St. Martin's Press, 1992), 75-76.

live rounds, one in his left lung and the other in the right chest wall which nicked the transverse scapular artery. He was taken to the nearest hospital, The Hospital for Sick Children in Great Ormond Street just a mile and a half from Covent Garden, where he died the following morning.

The second death was equally shocking, while adding scandal to the mix. It involved the suicide of Frances Murch, the eighteen-year-old amateur magician who Max von Leiden had begun featuring in his act.

Talk had been circulating in London society—the rumour mill again!—that the relationship of the magician and his young protégée was not as proper as it should have been. No one knew von Leiden's age (but the man applied blacking to his hair and goatee!). Whatever the man's age was, however, it was generally agreed that he had no business exploiting his fame and aura to take advantage of a girl Frances's age, especially one as shy as she was said to be.

Now the rumours were resurrected of the way von Leiden had touched the young female magician on stage as he was "assisting her" with a trick, or his odd habit of standing at an intimate distance behind her when he should have been off to the side. Those actions could be dismissed as inappropriate but understandable, however, in an older man working closely with someone in young womanhood.

What drew greater outrage was the ill treatment the magician had begun to confer on Frances Murch onstage. It had started with some gentle teasing over her name—initially her given name, then both her first and last name. When the tricks he was assigning her on stage didn't work (it was happening more and more because the illusions he let her try became harder), he not only didn't help in any way, but allowed the execution to fall flat, embarrassing the girl greatly.

Verbal abuse sometimes followed; and now and then von Leiden would become physically rough with her, though for the briefest of moments, and always when his body was positioned between the girl and the audience. There were times when she left the stage in tears. At those moments, von Leiden would turn to the audience and smile, or shrug, as if to say, "Well, I gave the little idiot a chance. Am I to blame because she fumbled the whole thing?"

Whether this treatment was enough to tip the scales, or more cruelty in the midst of a love affair between the two had driven her to despair, Frances Murch killed herself in the third week of May through an overdose of hydrate of chloral. Society decided that an abusive romantic relationship was most likely the cause, and Max von Leiden was universally blamed for his despicable and outrageous behavior.

But of course, no one could say that there *was* a love affair. There were also those who remarked that a little brusque behavior toward a young subordinate—of the type displayed in many sectors of society—certainly wasn't cause for suicide. Gradually, public opinion began to change. Frances Murch was probably unstable, poor girl. One could see how sudden fame could go to a young person's head. Perhaps she was in love with the renowned magician and couldn't accept his rejection of her. Surely *that* was a more reasonable assumption than to think that von Leiden would risk fame and fortune by taking up with someone who was (regrettably, it must be said), really nothing more than a shopgirl.

Frances Murch was buried in her parish churchyard two days after her suicide with only her family in attendance. The sun shone brilliantly, and the air was filled with the flowery scents of late May. No rain fell, and the sky didn't darken for a moment. Nature and London society both, it seemed, had more important things on their minds.

CHAPTER 9

Your Fondest Wish

hings had changed in the five weeks since Scarlet and Pierce-Jones had attended von Leiden's show. In April, the cabs waiting to discharge their passengers at the Queen Victoria Theatre Royal had been lined up and down the block along Haymarket Street. Tonight, the line curled around the corner onto Orange Street, and then down *that* block and onto Whitcomb Street.

Apparently, the Frances Murch scandal hadn't diminished enthusiasm for *Phantasmagoria*. Scarlet wondered if even standing-room-only tickets might be on sale; and when he and Django entered the theatre and he noticed patrons at the very back of the stalls, he saw that he was right.

By the start of the second act, he understood what the excitement was all about.

Until that point, *Phantasmagoria* consisted mostly of the same 'experiments' he and Django had seen five weeks ago: the wine into water trick, the spectacular electrical storm that nevertheless couldn't touch the people inside von Leiden's magic circle, and the seven-inch wax crocodile that became a *seven-foot-long* monster which 'devoured' a volunteer from the audience.

There was no goddess Ninlil this time, however, to be brought back from the dead to hover above the stage floor and answer questions from the audience. This time, the showstopper just before the curtain came down on the first act was an illusion (if it could be called that) which von Leiden called "The Invisible Orchestra."

Transforming himself into a conductor, he led an orchestra that could be heard but not seen. A delicate flick of the baton he was holding first elicited the lyrical strains of a violin emanating from somewhere up in the second balcony. A wind instrument (clarinet or oboe?) joined it from the other side of the first balcony. Theatregoers in both places could be seen looking at the seats around them, trying to see where the musicians were that they heard playing. But there were no musicians—only the sounds of, eventually, an entire invisible orchestra performing Mendelssohn's *Violin Concerto in E Minor*!

How was this possible? Scarlet thought of the graphophone, introduced just three years earlier by Alexander Graham Bell's company as an improvement on the phonograph. But like Edison's invention, the graphophone used wax-coated cylinders, which produced a small, tinny sound. The music that filled the Queen Victoria Theatre Royal now was loud and *alive,* exactly as if an orchestra were playing right on stage.

With a wave of his baton, Von Leiden stopped the music in mid-note, creating an ear-crushing silence. That lasted for ten seconds or so. Then applause exploded like a crack of thunder.

It was the perfect *tour de force* to bring down the curtain on Act One.

WHEN THE CURTAIN ROSE again the scene had been transformed. Except for twenty feet or so closest to the audience, the entire stage was now covered by a large curved blue scrim.[*] Unlit gas lights hung from the fly space behind the fabric, where presumably

---

[*] A *scrim* is a thinly woven curtain that appears solid when front-lit, but is transparent when a scene is lit from behind the fabric.

they would illuminate a scene performed in the now-empty space when they were lit.

Applause filled the theatre as soon as the curtain rose, even though there was no one on stage. Scarlet realized that the new setting must be a signal that tonight, von Leiden's most famous trick—the experiment he called "Your Fondest Wish"—would be performed. Apparently, the luck of the draw had favored him and Pierce-Jones.

When The Master of Illusion strode on stage, his energy level seemed doubled, as if he'd grown younger backstage during intermission. As soon as he reached center-stage he bowed deeply, acknowledging the reinvigorated applause which greeted his entrance. Then he waited patiently until the last pockets of it died away, holding the silence in his hand.

"Ladies and gentlemen—this is the moment you have all been waiting for. This is when you will discover not merely what life is . . . but what it can be!"

[Pause. The silence of the audience held.]

"*Is* life merely an illusion, as some claim? If that is so, we must look beyond the dream to discover reality itself. For I ask you: who is responsible for the life each of you has been living? It is not fate! It is not a supreme being with a magnificent beard living in a cloud! It is not even the forces of nature and biology as the men of science want you to believe.

"My friends—you are responsible for your own destiny. *And all you have to do is wish for it!*"

[Thunderous applause.]

"Tonight, in this theatre named after her majesty, your Queen, I will show you the way! You will see the events in the life of one of you pass before your eyes on stage—not only what has happened in this person's past, but *what is about to come*. Will I be performing a miracle? Perhaps. But it is a miracle you too can achieve in your own life. Tonight, I will show you how to throw off the shackles of your enslavement and create your own heaven!

"Ladies and gentlemen . . . learn how to live *Your Fondest Wish!*"

The applause was now joined by shouts and cheers. Scarlet and Pierce-Jones looked at each other. They were thinking the same thought: Does the man say this kind of thing every time he performs this trick? And if he does, why do the authorities allow the show to continue running? The level of sheer blasphemy displayed by The Master of Illusion was outrageous.

Von Leiden once again waited for the applause and acclamations to die down.

"Would one of you like to volunteer?"

[Laughter, some of it with a nervous edge.]

"Those that would, *stand up!*" commanded von Leiden, with his arms in the air and his hands flicking upward.

If half the audience didn't get to their feet, Scarlet would have been surprised. Now The Master himself, not one of his female assistants, left the stage to descend to the level of the patrons. The Queen Victoria Theatre Royal had no center aisle, so to create the effect he wanted, von Leiden circumnavigated the whole area encompassing the first-level stalls. He slowly traced the entire perimeter of 340 blue seats, walking slowly up one side aisle toward the back of the house and then down the opposite aisle back to the stage, looking the theatregoers over the entire time.

The audience held its breath.

Now he was standing dead-center, in front of the first row of seats at the patrons' level.

He thrust his arm out and pointed—not to the first-level stalls, not to the second-level Royal Circle, not even to the Upper Circle on the third floor. His finger was leveled at the gallery, the highest and cheapest section of the house with just seven rows. At this distance, no one could tell exactly where in that section he was indicating.

"You madam, in the long brown coat and flowered hat!"

Apparently, there was no doubt about whom von Leiden was referring to. Everyone in that section turned toward a woman who was standing in the next-to-last row. She looked left and right at the others in the row—all of whom were now staring at her—and placed one hand on her breast in the classic pose that said: "Do you mean me?" The magician nodded, exaggerating his head movement so it could be seen in almost literally the last row in the theatre, perhaps 60 feet above where he stood.

Despite everyone excitement, the audience waited patiently for the woman to make her way down three levels to the stage where The Master of Illusion now waited for her.

She was dressed as von Leiden had described her: in a long coat that reached almost to her ankles, light-brown in color, with six oversized buttons from the waist downward and gathered at the breast like a man's topcoat. The lady had on white gloves, and a large dome-shaped hat exactly the same color as her coat. The hat had a wide green cloth band decorated with artificial red and yellow berries (bittersweet?). She looked to be neither rich nor poor, but of the middle-class, perhaps slightly on the lower end of that scale. The audience had already placed her in their own minds as a governess or typist, and perhaps a widow.

According to what she now told von Leiden, her name was Margaret Sparrow, and she was 36 years old. She was indeed widowed, and had a son John ("Johnny"), aged eighteen.

This conversation, and the rest of it that followed, took place on the stage's apron, or the area in front of the large blue scrim that curved around to cover the entire space behind them. The magician had placed himself on stage right, or on the left side of the stage from the audience's perspective. That meant that when Margaret Sparrow joined him there, the two of them had cleared the sightlines so as not to obstruct anyone's view of the scrim. The area behind the thin curtain remained empty, the gas lights hanging above it still unlit.

"And Margaret, do you work outside the home?"

"Indeed, I do, sir. I'm a nurse at the Hanwell Asylum." A slight Scottish accent was revealing itself.

"Ah, excellent! Would you be so kind as to speak more loudly so the whole audience can hear you?"

The woman nodded.

"And tell us, Margaret, is that the institution also known as the Hanwell Pauper and Lunatic Asylum, and built for the pauper insane?"

The magician let just enough of the laughter which followed establish itself, before he held up his hand to stop it.

"Yes," said Margaret Sparrow in a slightly defensive voice. "But you know, in four days it's to be renamed as the London County Asylum."

"Extraordinary! To think that I selected you as our volunteer tonight without knowing that that was the case! Did I know you before this so that I singled you out deliberately?"

"No, sir. We've never met before."

"Thank you. And your son—I believe you said his name is John. Where is he?"

"He's in the army, sir. The First Battalion of the Grenadier Guards," she added proudly.

"Ah, he's a big lad then?"

"Aye."

"Serving where at the moment?"

"The Sudan."

"I see. In the Mahdist Wars. A nasty business, that. I hope he comes home safely."

Before the woman could reply, the magician asked her, though he turned to face the audience:

"And have you any objection to being mesmerized?"

The woman nodded. Then realizing that that would be confusing, that what was really needed was a negative response which actually meant yes, she said: "I mean, no sir. I have no objection."

"Because you realize that you won't be able to participate in this experiment otherwise?"

[More laughter.]

"Enough, then." And in the booming voice which effortlessly filled the theatre: "LET US BEGIN!"

He started on the mesmeric passes. Instructing Mrs. Sparrow to close her eyes, he placed his right hand with the palm almost but not quite touching her solar plexus. He left the hand there for some time, not moving it at all as he watched his subject's face. Then he went behind her and placed his fingers on the closed eyes, with a thumb resting on each cheekbone (what Scarlet would have called the infraorbital foramen).

Gently, first in one direction then the other, the magician rotated Mrs. Sparrow's head. Placing himself in front of her again, he made gliding passes with both hands downwards and outwards, as though he were "sweeping" away any old energies that remained inside her. Now, from in front, he placed his fingertips at each of the woman's temples, leaving them motionless there as again he studied her face with a penetrating gaze.

Then something almost imperceptible happened. But Scarlet's medically-trained mind saw it. (Asking Pierce-Jones afterward, he learned that the other hadn't perceived it at all.)

Von Leiden's fingertips were still placed on Mrs. Sparrow's temples when she jerked perceptibly, as though an electrical shock passed through her. A second or two passed; then she seemed to tighten all over and to shake slightly. It seemed to Scarlet that the magician's hands were pressing more tightly now against the temples, as if he was controlling what was happening.

The idea of a grand mal seizure arose in his mind, but he dismissed it. This was something else: a deep and steady excitation—not one that rose to a crescendo like an epileptic fit. Whatever energy was coursing through the woman, it was steady and unchanging. He leaned forward in his seat to see all of this more clearly, and thought he saw Margaret Sparrow's eyes open slightly for a moment. But he was too far away from the stage to know for sure. He glanced quickly around him, but no one else was reacting in any way. Mrs. Sparrow was standing placidly now with her eyes closed, and Scarlet wondered whether he had actually seen her reaction or had just imagined it.

Von Leiden repeated the sweeping movement with his arms and

hands, though this time in the opposite direction. The arms swept upward and toward Margaret Sparrow's head, as though he were directing energy *toward* the subject instead of ridding her of it.

A long moment went by as von Leiden simply watched the mesmerized woman standing absolutely still on stage with her eyes closed. Then, the gas lights behind the scrim flamed on, and the bare stage below them became visible.

Now the magician began asking Mrs. Sparrow a series of questions:

"Where were you born?"

"What was your family like?"

"When did you come to London?"

"When did you first fall in love? What did you feel?"

And an instruction: "Tell me what it is like at the Hanwell Asylum."

As she stood on stage and answered each question, people entered the area behind the scrim and *began acting out what Mrs. Sparrow was describing*. From the clothes they wore and the setting that appeared on stage, the locale could have been Scotland. But there was no doubt that they were performing in a silent mime the things the mesmerized woman was describing.

First, a family scene: a mother and father and six children, a domestic scene inside a house, then the children running outside to play. To Scarlet, these people somehow didn't look like adult and child actors. They looked *real*.

Whatever this strange enactment could be, it was extraordinary to watch. With each question and answer, the people behind the scrim changed based on what Margaret Sparrow was saying. All of it had the dreamlike quality that scenes enacted behind a translucent curtain are invested with. After the domestic scene, a crowded street in London with the jumble of humanity one finds here. Then a tender scene between two young lovers—with a girl who looked exactly like a younger Margaret Sparrow! And, last and most incredible, a scene presumably from Hanwell Asylum in the present: the elderly naked patients lying on the floor; the screamers—horribly silent but with all the physical gestures of despair; the preeners who paraded in front of everyone (some of whom were naked too); and the lost souls, rocking endlessly back and forth.

The *Phantasmagoria* audience watched all of this in silent fascination. Then the gas lights abruptly went out, and the area behind the curtain was plunged into sudden darkness. Everyone's attention naturally returned to the magician and the audience volunteer.

"But all of this is past," The Master of Illusion reminded his audience. He turned to the woman standing beside him. "It is time to create your own destiny. . . . Mrs. Margaret Sparrow—*what is your fondest wish?*"

"It is to have my son, my Johnny, come home to me."

There had been no hesitation, no attempt at drama. The statement was so plain and simple that one knew it had to hold great emotion and the deepest of intentions.

"Then you shall have your wish!"

The lights behind the scrim flared up again to reveal two people on stage. In the far corner in front of the theatre's back wall—as though he'd just entered the building itself—stood a tall young man dressed in a Grenadier Guards uniform. In the resplendent dress uniform of scarlet jacket, white belt, black trousers with the red stripe, and sleeves with black cuffs and large gold buttons (though without the enormous bearskin hat), the lad stood proudly. Standing where he was looking was *another* Margaret Sparrow—not the one with The Master of Illusion, turned toward the audience with her eyes still closed.

With a look of joy, the other Mrs. Sparrow extended her right arm toward the young solider. The two of them began moving toward each other, uncertainly at first, then more quickly. Exactly in counterpoint (it seemed), the gas lights behind the scrim began to fade, as the upstage area slowly went to black.

Von Leiden bowed his head for a moment as if exhausted.

Margaret Sparrow had opened her eyes and now looked slightly dazed, though no longer mesmerized.

Now the rafters of the theatre shook with the explosion of applause that erupted. The entire crowd was standing, with people all around them yelling. Pierce-Jones leaned over and shouted above the din:

"It's said that the person mesmerized will now achieve their wish just as was shown on stage!"

Scarlet frowned.

"Said by *whom!*"

"I don't know! I've heard lots of rumours though! . . . Bravo! Bravissimo!"

"Well, it is quite an illusion."

"What do you mean, old man! It's magic!"

Scarlet, the amateur actor, had a sudden irrational thought. He would race down the aisle before anyone left their seat and make his way backstage. There, in the corridors and costumer's shop and dressing rooms, he would find the actors, taking off their costumes and removing their makeup—all of the performers who had just acted out the scenes of Margaret Sparrow's life behind the scrim. He would see them for the stage professionals and child-performers they were. Not the actual people from Mrs. Sparrow's past. Of course not! All of this was clever stage direction, not magic!

But he didn't do it. Not because he was afraid of what he would find when he looked in those places where actors can be found after the final curtain.

At least, he didn't think that was the reason he stayed where he was, applauding with all the rest.

CHAPTER 10

J.N. Maskelyne

The world of the theatre—like any *demimonde*—is a small one.

Only one of the students Scarlet had worked with in amateur dramatics at Oxford had gone on to a career in the professional theatre. ("Young men don't attend university to become actor-vagabonds," the banker father of one of his friends had reminded his son when the lad had broached the idea.)

Leonard Golding certainly hadn't done any such thing. Instead, he had become an impresario: a producer of entertainments. The word could also mean the owner of a theatre where these productions took place. In Leonard's case, it meant both. He was not only a promoter of stage shows, but the owner of—at last count—nine theatres known collectively in the United Kingdom as the Golding Organization.

These days, magic shows were a more important part than ever of the acts booked into London's temples of culture like the Golding theatres. Which was why Scarlet found himself walking into his old friend's office in Irving Street in Leicester Square.

He had asked not to be announced, for he was looking forward to the expression on the other man's face when he saw who had just come through the door. The producer-owner was writing something, with his head down and a serious look on his face.

Scarlet stopped, accepting the momentary advantage that was his to take a good look at his friend.

Dapper had been the word for Leonard Golding from his college days onward. He was the kind of man who dressed impeccably, even fussily, every day, whether it was a work day or not. Even at university this was true. In those days, he could invariably be found in the audience, taking notes in the rehearsals of the plays he directed. You would never find him up on stage in shirtsleeves, walking around on a never-washed and seldom swept stage (the female members of a cast always wore rehearsal skirts). Leonard's suits also changed with the season in terms of colors and the weight of the fabric—behavior which was astonishing to the other young men in the Dramatic Society, nearly all of whom came from wealthy families but disdained to show it.

Today, in honor of spring, Leonard's suit was a shade of grey his tailor had called *flint*, his waistcoat a more subtle grey the man had labeled *coin*. The ascot was, heretically for an Englishman, a shade known as *Yale blue*. Striped grey trousers (alas, of a shade known in the trade merely as "grey") completed his ensemble. Scarlet couldn't see Leonard's shoes from where he stood, but they were surely black and polished to a mirror shine.

Something made Golding look up from his writing. He tossed the pen onto the paper and leaped to his feet and crossed to Scarlet all in one quick fluid motion.

"Will Scarlet! You bloody rascal, you're looking younger than ever," he said and extended his hand. "Another decade, and I'll be kissing your cheek and slapping your behind, or the other way around."

Scarlet laughed. It was something Golding just might do, especially if there was an audience to witness it.

"Come sit, sit. Drink?"

"Whisky?"

"Of course. Ice? Water? Okay, neat." Then, turning back to Scarlet after attending to the drinks: "By God, it's good to see you!

How long's it been? Never mind. Have a bloody drink and catch me up."

"You're looking well," said Scarlet, accepting the glass. "Do you have news of a wife and kiddies to tell me about yet?"

"Like bloody hell. With all the shows I put on or book into my houses, and all the pretty young things interested in meeting the producer?"

Scarlet listened for any compensating regret that might have been present in Leonard's voice. But he didn't hear any.

"How about you? Still with Scotland Yard?"

"Scalpel and badge in hand—in that order."

"Busy?"

"By God."

And the two men nodded at the accuracy of that statement for both of them.

"Go on, sit," Golding repeated, and when Scarlet had done so, rolled his chair from behind the desk so that it was next to his friend's.

"I keep hearing about all your successful shows," Scarlet said. "And your theatres always seem to have tenants."

"Then I won't show you my master calendar. Or my books, for heaven's sake. I'll leave you in blissful ignorance of what a harum-scarum business this is. But listen, you dog—why the visit? Do you have something on your mind?"

"As a matter of fact, I do," replied Scarlet. There was no need to play ring a ring o' roses with an old friend like this. "I'm hoping that with your position, you could refer me to someone I might talk to."

"About what?"

"Magic."

"Ah. Looking for a new profession after all the crime and blood and guts?"

Scarlet smiled. "Not a bad idea, now that you mention it. Actually, I'm looking into an act, and before I go any further, I'd like to have something of a foundation for what's being done. In terms of the illusions, I mean."

Leonard Golding considered this response. "Since you didn't say, 'I'm *investigating* an act,' I take it that this is unofficial."

"Yes, it is."

"Whose show is it we're talking about?

"Max von Leiden, The Master of Illusion."

"*Phantasmagoria?*"

"Exactly."

"It's not one of my shows, you know."

"Yes, I know that."

Golding thought for a moment. "There *is* someone you can talk to—someone I've booked many times over. He's one of the best in the business. I'm sure he'd be willing to talk to you. His name is John Nevil Maskelyne, but he goes by J.N. Ever hear of him?"

"No. Is he famous?"

"Extremely. He's the inventor of the Levitation trick, which he started performing about twenty years ago. If you'd ever seen that illusion performed, you'd be bloody amazed, I can tell you. He's about sixty now, and still going strong." He thought about it some more. "Yes, he's the one you should talk to."

He wrote something on a notepad, then tore off the sheet and handed it to Scarlet. After some reminiscing, and a secretary's entrance to remind the impresario about some pressing matters, the two of them stood, began to shake hands, then gave it up and hugged each other. They made the usual statements about not taking so long to get in touch next time.

"And Will?" said Golding as Scarlet was at the door. "Be bloody careful, wherever this leads you. Von Leiden isn't the man to cross."

"Not to worry," said Scarlet with a smile.

"No, I'm serious, old man. Don't fuck with this fellow."

———————

SCARLET GAVE HORACE BILBY[*] the task of compiling some information for him on Mr. J.N. Maskelyne, magician and inventor of the Levitation illusion. As soon as he received the packet in return, he realized that the assignment must have been a mere jaunt for Bilby's firm, and probably assigned to a junior clerk.

For Maskelyne was a famous magician indeed. For sixteen years, he had been resident at Egyptian Hall in Piccadilly, well known as a mecca for magicians who gave lectures and performances there. He was also a member of The Magic Circle, the British institution dedicated to advancing the art of magic.

Maskelyne had gained fame at the age of just sixteen in 1855— at the height of the spiritualist mania in England—when he and a fellow conjurer recreated and debunked the Davenport Brothers' act with its fake supernaturalism. He was not only a performer, but a prolific inventor who held numerous patents. (Three years from now, in 1892, he would invent a penny-operated toilet, single-handedly creating the English euphemism, "to spend a penny.")

Apart from inventing the Levitation trick, Maskelyne was also the creator of Psycho. Psycho was a twenty-two-inch tall automaton dressed as a Hindu boy who sat on a raised cushion above the floor, so all could see that he wasn't operated from below by any wires or pullies. Psycho could not only add and subtract numbers—he could also spell out words, enjoy a cigarette, and compete in a game of whist!

The two men met at Egyptian Hall three days after Scarlet's chat with Leonard Golding. At first, he had thought that his old college chum's business card, along with Golding's importance as a theatre owner who booked magic acts, was the reason Maskelyne had agreed

---

[*]Horace Bilby was a fussy gentleman of indeterminate age, known to Scarlet and Pierce-Jones as The Reader. He was the founder of a private concern—England's best—offering discreet and in-depth research of existing records on any organization or individual. See *Red Season*, Book #1 in the Dr. William Scarlet Mysteries.

to meet with him. But he found the man to be charming, gracious, and intelligent. He had a thick wave of dark hair combed straight back from the forehead and a walrus mustache, and looked back at Scarlet with a steady placid look in his eyes. Neither the hair nor the mustache showed any grey, despite the man's fifty-nine years.

It was late afternoon (Maskelyne was performing that night at the Hall), and the magician had led Scarlet to a comfortable space with walls painted in a welcoming and lively coral red. Judging by the mirror, makeup pots and chair, and the costumes hanging on a rack next to those items, this was apparently a combination sitting room, dressing room, and makeup room.

Maskelyne had placed two mismatched salon chairs so they faced each other, one covered in a lined fabric of light tan, the other in a hideous green floral material. He sat now with one leg crossed and the opposite arm draped over the back of his chair (the hideous one), his pose as casual and unstudied as his decidedly crooked tie.

Scarlet had introduced himself before the two men sat, and his host had asked after their mutual acquaintance, Leonard Golding. The Scotland Yard surgeon-detective now realized he didn't quite know how to begin to explain the reason for his visit. He found himself falling back on the standard police opening, though that wasn't at all the impression he wanted to convey.

"How well do you know Max von Leiden, sir?"

"'John,' please. Just as a fellow professional. A very fine magician."

"Yes, I've seen his show *Phantasmagoria* twice."

"What did you think?"

Scarlet hesitated, then said: "Unbelievable."

"In what sense?"

And with that, Scarlet realized that they were already into it. He found a tightness in his shoulders that he hadn't realized was there letting go.

"That's really what I'm here to ask you about . . . John. I'm trying to understand how some of the illusions in von Leiden's show *are* magic tricks. Excuse me, I know that doesn't make sense. But I'm hoping you can give me some insight into how illusions like these are accomplished."

"Without actually asking me how the tricks are done, though."

"Oh, yes. I'm sorry. Did you think—?"

"Actually, I didn't," replied J.N. Maskelyne. "People are always asking that, though, as you may guess. And no magician who's worth his salt will ever tell them." He leaned over to lift a small box from a nearby table and opened the lid.

"Cigarette?"

"No, thank you."

Maskelyne lit his and leaned back in the chair, this time with both hands on his lap.

"Which illusions do you have in mind?"

Scarlet didn't want to begin with the two 'experiments' that he was most bothered by. So he started small.

"Well, the wine into water trick."

"Oh, yes. That one is as old as the hills, and there isn't any great secret behind it. For the magician, that is. Two decanters sit on a table, one filled with a clear liquid—which we are told is water; and the other with a red liquid—which we are informed is wine. The magician announces he will turn one into the other. He waves a large scarf or other cloth in front of the table, keeps it there for a short time, and when he takes it away: Voila! The water has turned into wine, and vice-versa. Is that how von Leiden is performing it?"

"Yes, that's it exactly."

"In this case, I'll reveal what's really happening. As I say, there aren't any trade secrets involved here. Each carafe has a hole in the bottom, you see, that is filled with a plug of wax. They also have a transparent chamber at the top that's filled with water, which of course you cannot see."

"But the containers are glass!"

"You mean, how can they have a hole in the bottom? It's simplicity itself to drill a hole in a glass bottle if you know what you're doing. While the scarf hides what's being done, the magician takes out the plug in both containers, and the liquid inside them flows into a hidden compartment in the table. He then quickly releases the water from the transparent compartment in each decanter into its main chamber. In whichever carafe had the 'water' last time, he drops a pellet he has concealed in his hand which turns the liquid red. Of course, he'd better remember which was white and which was red previously. Then he whisks away the concealing scarf, and you have a transfiguration of the liquids."

"And you say this is an old trick?"

"Ancient. Von Leiden gives it a religious twist though, doesn't he? Says something about the miracle he'll be performing—turning wine into water—which is the opposite of the 'trick' performed at the wedding in Galilee?"

"Exactly."

Scarlet thought about the explanation of the trick.

"I see. It's simple when you know how it's done, isn't it?"

"*Every* illusion in a magic show is simple—even obvious, if your frame of mind is what it should be. But of course, it's the magician's job to either misdirect you or make you rely on the wrong set of perceptions. The utter simplicity of magic is a big reason that magicians never reveal their secrets. They know everyone will immediately become blasé and find the thing boring. Or they will tell themselves they're stupid for not seeing such an obvious solution. It's not a frame of mind you want to get your audience into."

"Fair enough. I swear I'll never do it again."

The two men shared a laugh.

"You said a few minutes ago that you want to know 'how the illusions are accomplished.' What did you mean if it's not how the tricks are carried out?"

Scarlet thought about how he could put into words what he was feeling. It didn't help that he was not sure of the latter himself.

"It's not the mechanics of the tricks I'm asking out. I mean the sleight of hand, or even the contraptions used, like those specially designed decanters."

"What, then?"

"Well, you see . . . I'm really interested if an illusion isn't an illusion at all, but something different."

"You mean reality."

"Not exactly. . . . Look, take the theatre. When you watch a play, you realize it isn't reality at all. But there aren't any tricks being performed to fool you." He thought about that. "I guess you're fooling yourself. It's a convention, you see: the acceptance of certain things you're seeing and hearing *as if* they were actually happening. In the theatre, it's called 'the willing suspension of disbelief.' Well, what if it were larger than that? Something we might call, I don't know, the willing suspension of the way the world works?"

"Sorry. I don't follow."

"Let's see. . . . What if everyone in an audience, or any group for that matter, was willing to be deceived about reality? What if they *wanted* to be deceived in that way?"

Maskelyne raised his eyebrows and shrugged.

"Then you're on thin ice, aren't you, old boy? You'd first have to define reality before you can determine what everyone is either buying into or reacting against. And that's a bloody impossible task, isn't it?"

"Yes, I suppose it is. So, you're saying that magic shows aren't fair game for questions like these?"

"Actually, the opposite. They're the perfect situations to ask these questions about. Magicians exploit people's willingness for self-deception—in a harmless way, and only for the purposes of entertainment. It's why they despise the charlatans who claim some supernatural agency in their acts. Some magicians come right out and tell audiences at the beginning of their shows that there's nothing dark or occult concerning what they're about to see—it's all for fun and entertainment. And really, it is."

"And what if one doesn't believe that it *is* an act of self-deception on an audience's part?" said Scarlet. Again, he had the feeling that he should apologize for an absurd line of thinking.

Maskelyne eyed him shrewdly. Scarlet had the sudden thought: *All magicians are psychologists.*

"You're thinking about von Leiden again, aren't you? Are you asking if his biggest experiments *are* illusions?"

Scarlet felt that arrow hit its mark.

"Yes. There are two of them I keep wondering about—the finales of the shows I attended. Do you know the illusion where von Leiden summons an ancient princess of Arabia or somewhere? I don't remember her name."

"I haven't seen it. But I know of it."

"It's the upper body of a woman who hovers in mid-air above the stage and answers questions about the future. Von Leiden asked her about British foreign policy, for goodness sake. And she replied! How can you explain that?"

"I can't," answered Maskelyne. "There are some illusions from top magicians that the rest of us haven't been able to figure out. Sometimes, we get fairly close with a version we cook up, but apart from espionage there's no way we can know." He smiled. "There are one or two of my own experiments that are in that category."

Scarlet nodded, but his mind was already on the second illusion.

"Have you seen 'Your Fondest Wish'?" Before Maskelyne could answer, he added: "Is it done with . . . what do you call them, plants in the audience? Are the volunteers coached before they're called on stage?"

"No, it isn't, and they aren't," Maskelyne replied flatly.

"Can you be sure?"

"Yes, I can. In this business, we know if a magician is doing what you're describing. It's not unheard of, of course. But no really good conjurer does it. And we always know. I can tell you with certainty that Max von Leiden doesn't use plants for 'Your Fondest Wish.'"

"Then how is it done? Supposedly, the audience volunteer is mesmerized, and then answers questions from his or her life. And *immediately*, those scenes start unfolding behind the scrim, with people acting out what the mesmerized person is describing. As soon as they answer a new question, a new scene arises, showing exactly how that too supposedly happened in real life."

"And you're thinking it's impossible for such a recreation to actually be taking place on stage?"

"It *is* impossible," answered Scarlet. "The actors, the blocking, the staging, the hue of the lights on stage changing to the new scene. None of it could be done in the time between the question being answered and that part of the person's past life being acted out. It happens virtually simultaneously. And then, *this person's future is shown*! How does our pretty argument about self-deception and reality versus illusion come into play in something like that?"

J.N. Maskelyne leaned forward in his chair, so that his clasped hands were only inches from the other man's knees.

"You have no idea, Mr. Scarlet, how often those same questions have been asked about von Leiden's most famous illusion at The Magic Circle. Yes, and in many other places and at other times in my profession.

"We simply have no answers. You see us as professionals, and we are—the very best in our chosen way of life. But sometimes with a really great magician, an illusion defies our efforts to work it out. And I'm afraid that Max von Leiden's 'Your Fondest Wish' is in that category."

It would be trite to say that at this moment, Scarlet was having trouble recognizing reality versus an illusion. But he felt that way.

At any rate, J.N. Maskelyne had a performance to prepare for. He thanked Scarlet for the visit, and handed him a pair of tickets for one of his upcoming shows.

Waiting for a cab outside Egyptian Hall a few minutes later, Scarlet was glad he'd visited the great magician to get at the truths behind The Master of Illusion's show.

Even if his fondest wish hadn't come true.

CHAPTER 11

Twelve Questions

[Scene: That evening, a Thursday. The location is the dining room of Django Pierce-Jones's house in Grosvenor Square. Scarlet and Pierce-Jones are having dinner.]

DJANGO.
He sounds like an interesting fellow.

SCARLET.
Yes, he is. Quite intelligent and knowledgeable. Very generous with his time as well. I understand he's extremely well thought of among other magicians.

DJANGO.
And it sounds like he gave you some interesting insights.

SCARLET.
I suppose so. As much as he could, given what I was asking. I can't help thinking it's much larger than that, though.

DJANGO.
How do you mean?

SCARLET.
I mean something that goes beyond what von Leiden may have done in these cases.

DJANGO.
I don't follow you, old man. What cases?

SCARLET.
Giuseppe Caliosto and Frances Murch.

DJANGO.
Frances . . . Oh, the young girl who committed suicide—the amateur magician von Leiden was including in his act. What do she and the late great Marco the Magnificent have to do with any of it?

SCARLET.
Well, why do you think I'm looking into Max von Leiden?

DJANGO.
I assumed you've suddenly become consumed with these magic shows. It certainly seems that way. And that you may have had a psychometric vision—though why you wouldn't tell me about it, I have no idea. Is something else going on?

SCARLET [*laughing*].
Let's hope that my suddenly becoming infatuated with magic is what von Leiden thinks as well. And no, I haven't had a vision through my psychometry.

DJANGO.
What, then?

SCARLET.

Think about it, Django. A master magician dies performing a trick he's done hundreds of times. And an eighteen-year-old girl kills herself after being abused. Do you detect a link here?

DJANGO.

I see. Does Mallinson* know you're interested in the man?

SCARLET.

Do you think he'd sanction an investigation of a world-famous magician on nothing but my gut instinct?

DJANGO.

Point taken. All right. You suspect that von Leiden may be implicated in the Caliosto and Murch cases. Are you also thinking that there may be something else he's trying to hide?

SCARLET.

That's what I'm trying to find out. Interested in helping me?

DJANGO.

Is Victoria the Queen of England?

---

* Sir Edward Mallinson, M.D., Chief Surgeon of the Metropolitan Police (Scotland Yard), and Scarlet's superior.

CHAPTER 12

The Death of Oliver Wyatt

carlet's weekday morning hours at his home surgery were always slowest on Fridays. Patients tended to put off until the following week any ailments or injuries that didn't need immediate attention.

This morning, the thirty-first of May, was even more so, given the lovely weather outside. He actually had some free time between his fourth and fifth patients, which he used for some quick research. He rapidly scoured É. Robin's 1854 book, *Causes Générales de la Vieillesse de la Mor Senile et du Développement de la Taille dans les Animaux* (*General Causes of Aging, Senile Death and Size Development in Animals*).

He had just enough time to also learn about Mauritian physiologist Charles-Édouard Brown-Séquard's article, just published in *Seances de la Societe de Biologie* (*Meetings of the Biological Society*) entitled "Des effets produits chez l'homme par des injections sous-cutanées d'un liquid retire des testicules frais de cobaye et de chien" ("Effects in man of subcutaneous injections of freshly prepared liquid from guinea pig and dog testes").

He was looking for any information concerning the rapid-aging disease he had encountered twice now. The first time had been the visit to his surgery on April 5th of Mrs. Walter Keeley-Campbell. His autopsy of sixteen-year-old Charlotte Tibbins, just eighteen days later, had revealed a second case of extreme and inexplicable early senescence. Scarlet was calling the condition, strictly for his own purposes, *Senecta Syndrome* (old-age syndrome).

He had no idea that the next patient on his schedule this morning would show all the signs of the disease.

In this case, Scarlet didn't have to ask the patient's name. It was Oliver Wyatt—the dissolute rogue who was always in the news concerning his scandalous lifestyle and escapades amid London's high society.

He had seen the young man's photograph enough times, and glimpsed him on the street or at social events to recognize him immediately now. Unfortunately, however, Wyatt could no longer be described as a 'young man.'

The shrunken fellow he was shaking hands with now might have been Wyatt's great-grandfather, if that gentleman had still been alive. All of the well-known features were there. But now they were weirdly transformed.

It was one thing for Scarlet to have met a woman for the first time two months ago who looked very old but claimed to be only forty-six. It was quite another to be looking into a famous visage that had been shockingly changed into something out of Edgar Allan Poe or Hieronymus Bosch.

Even the man's stature was greatly reduced—due no doubt to muscle atrophy and loss of bone mass. Wyatt was known to be slightly over six feet in height. Yet now, Scarlet found himself next to someone who was perceptibly shorter than his own five-eleven-and-a-half inches. The expensive clothes hung on this man like a discarded suit on a scarecrow.

The famous placid and unlined face was greatly changed. Once perfectly oval-shaped and delicate to the point of prettiness, it now sagged everywhere as folds of flesh dragged it down. The eyes, once clear and arrogant, were now only glimpsed under heavy lids—and in fact, the left eye could be described as partially closed. Half-circles of pouchy flesh as big as scallop shells hung below those eyes.

The long nose now dominated the facial structure as never before—marching forward as the midface around and behind it became hollowed out. The buccinator muscles at either side of the mouth had almost completely let go, causing the well-known devil-may-care look of the pouty lips to become downturned, dour, and pessimistic-looking.

Deep lines traversed this face where once there had been none: in the nasolabial folds between the giant nose and mouth; in marionette lines leading from the corner of the lips to the chin; and everywhere on the droopy forehead and brows. The thick flowing brown hair (known to be touched up to cover up premature grayness) was now white. Whatever was happening to Wyatt had evidently been enough to make him leave off dyeing it.

Despite his appearance, Scarlet was expecting a *bon mot* from the famous wit. But when they shook hands, all that Wyatt said (as far as Scarlet could hear it through the mumbling), was an entirely conventional, "How do you do, sir?"

"Please have a seat," Scarlet instructed his patient, indicating a chair. He had a fleeting thought of Scrooge's same instruction to the ghost of Marley in *A Christmas Carol*, and then adding: "Can you sit down?"

Wyatt could.

Though the next question was superfluous, Scarlet had to ask it.

"What can I do for you, sir?"

This time there was no mumbling. His voice shaking with passion, Oliver Wyatt said: "You can bring me out of hell, Dr. William Scarlet. Can you do that?"

"Are you referring to—?"

"Of course, I'm referring to!" Wyatt straightened up in the chair, wincing from what must be a severely arthritic spine.

"Do you know how old I am, sir? I'm twenty-four. *Twenty-four!* Would you have guessed it, looking at me?"

Scarlet simply side-stepped the question, which wasn't one at all.

"Have any other doctors advised you in this case? I imagine that someone in your position . . ."

"Ah—you mean Harley Street. The best of the best, is it? — The most brilliant medical minds the Empire has to offer. I would do better by visiting a shaman. No, I've had enough of them. I've heard of your work in unexplainable cases—never mind how—and here I am. I need someone who knows how to look into unusual causes for diseases, and I'm told that's your specialty. For the love of God, man, *look at me!*"

Scarlet resisted the urge to reach out and cover one of the man's hands with his own. It simply wasn't done. And he doubted whether a patient in this state would respond positively. Such a gesture might be welcomed in the next stage—resignation—but not yet. The truth was, he doubted whether a man with Wyatt's well-known mocking state of mind would tolerate it in any of the stages he was destined to go through.

Wyatt's anger and impatience were actually liberating, Scarlet realized. He would be able to ask his questions without the inconvenience of having to perpetually soften them for the patient.

"When did your symptoms begin?"

"In January of this year."

Good Lord, though Scarlet: *He's talking about four months!*

A soft chuckle escaped Wyatt. "Oddly enough, last year was wonderful. Everything had been going well for me. And one day, I became winded while walking in St. James Park. That's how it began."

"Had you experienced a prior illness of any kind?"

"Just the opposite. I was feeling at my best. Before you ask: I had been drinking as I always do. My drinking is excessive, of course. Well, I mustn't be modest. It's monumental. But that's always been the case over the last six years or so. And nothing in my lifestyle could account for what happened next."

"What do you mean?"

"I mean, going from needing to catch my breath while walking, to being severely arthritic and breathless within two months. I've become horribly stiff in my legs, hands, and neck especially. You see how I have to hold myself just sitting here, don't you? And then . . . everything on the outside began visibly aging. I take it you're not of society, Doctor. But I haven't been out of my house for a month, which for me is simply a scandal. There was a brouhaha at the end of April concerning a certain house and some pretty friends of mine, when I was hauled into court. Did you happen to read about it in the papers?"

"Well . . . "

"Yes, of course, you did. Up until then I had been masking my symptoms as well as I could. — You have no idea of the value of good makeup and bad lighting, Doctor.

Naturally, I had to continue making my rounds of the clubs and . . . other places. But I became very good at sitting in corners and the darkest parts of rooms. Then the molly house raid happened and we were all arrested. The judge, dressed like Death himself in one of those awful black robes, released us all until sentencing, which gave me the excuse I needed to go into hiding." The voice became more serious. "Whatever is happening to me was accelerating, you see."

"So, you decided to seek medical help."

"Obviously."

"And you haven't yet been under any doctor's care?"

"You already asked—" began Wyatt, but started coughing. The cough began with a harsh sound in the throat, but then became deeper, until it fairly boomed from the chest.

Scarlet waited for the coughing to subside so that he could begin his examination. He wanted, among other things, to check the lung sounds and whether the airways were clear.

Suddenly, Wyatt's upper torso heaved forward, as a much more violent cough racked him. He took a deep gasping breath—and with the next cough, blood exploded out of his mouth and splashed everywhere. Then his eyes dulled, he seemed to fold into himself, and he fell out of the chair and into the red slippery puddle on the floor.

It was a massive hemoptysis—a pulmonary hemorrhage. Scarlet immediately yelled for help from his assistant Archibald Hunt in the next room, and knelt beside Wyatt, who had lost all alertness.

His first task in a case of hemoptysis of this severity was to determine whether the bleeding was of gastrointestinal or pulmonary origin. But looking at the floor around him, he realized that it didn't matter. Wyatt had suddenly produced what looked to Scarlet to be twenty ounces or more of blood. Coughing up that much blood *in a twenty-four hour period* is considered fatal; and Wyatt had done it in a single spasm. The protocol now went from etiology—determining the origin of the condition—to dealing with the immediate trauma.

Given the breathing problems Wyatt had described earlier, Scarlet suspected bronchiectasis, or thickening and damage to the walls of the bronchi. But again, the critical issue at this moment was to clear Wyatt's airways.

He was hoping to get the patient stable. But considering what was happening, and the look of the man lying in a pool of his own blood, he knew that the odds were slim even for that. Now Hunt, Scarlet's assistant, ran into the room and immediately knelt beside the doctor and patient.

"Hold him up from the shoulders," Scarlet ordered.

Wyatt was still coughing, his body heaving up weakly with each effort of his lungs to clear the blood, which was bubbling up out of his mouth. The coughing stopped. Then with one last, pronounced exhalation, the body settled into Hunt's arms and the light that was in the eyes went out.

Oliver Wyatt, the darling and bad-boy of London society—the rich aristocratic libertine who was always good for a salacious headline and a whispered scandal—was dead.

Scarlet looked at Wyatt's face, which had the look of total exhaustion which has finally given way, and wondered what the obituary notices in the newspapers would say. One thing was certain: they could never print the truth about the awful and baffling new condition that had killed the man:

Oliver Wyatt, the 24-year-old wit and bon vivant who constantly captured the press's attention, died today at the estimated age of 90. Unfortunately, before the vicar at the church service could say, "dust to dust," Wyatt already was.

THE LAST PATIENTS OF the day in Scarlet's surgery were rescheduled to appointments in the following week. In the absence of a suspicious or violent death, and as procedure dictated, someone at one of the nearby hospitals would be assigned to perform the autopsy.

To Scarlet, it didn't matter.

He already knew what that doctor would find.

CHAPTER 13

The Methuselah Plague

nd now the mysterious rapid-aging disease(?) spread. Since no discernible crime was being committed, it was not officially any business of Scotland Yard. But of course, it was the common business. And so Scarlet and his fellow physicians were just as concerned and baffled as everyone else.

The contagion (if that's what it should be called) was miniscule in terms of civilization's afflictions. At the last count, there were only a few dozen cases in the entire country. In France, Germany, and the United States—the other nations affected—the total of cases reached no more than two hundred.

Everywhere, the symptoms were precisely what Scarlet had witnessed personally in the three cases he'd been involved with: Mrs. Walter Keely-Campbell, Charlotte Tibbins, and Oliver Wyatt. In every case, premature aging of unknown origin occurred suddenly and proceeded with astonishing speed. Within the space of only three or four months, affected individuals progressed from normal and robust health to decrepit versions of themselves. Incredibly, once the disease had manifested itself, those stricken aged an average of *twenty years for each month they lived.*

Frantic efforts were launched at England and Scotland's major hospitals and medical schools to identify the mysterious condition. But every effort was stymied by the fact that the patients being examined died too quickly. Every avenue explored—from physical examinations to blood tests to investigations of family histories to autopsies—ended with the same frustrating diagnosis: these people had died of simple old age.

But old age not simply arrived at.

In the midst of their frustration, doctors and scientists at least gave the terrible affliction a name.

They were calling it The Methuselah Plague.

SCARLET SUDDENLY HAD TIME on his hands. His contribution to the research on The Methuselah Plague consisted of making his notes on Mrs. Keely-Campbell and Oliver Wyatt's office visits available, and sharing his autopsy findings on Charlotte Tibbins. There was nothing like the Jack the Ripper frenzy of seven months ago to clear everyone's desk at the Yard and send them to Whitechapel looking desperately for clues. He could turn his full attention to Max von Leiden's connection with the deaths of Giuseppe Caliosto and Frances Murch.

Any such investigation would have to be outside his official capacity as an assistant surgeon of the Metropolitan Police, of course. His superior, Chief Surgeon Sir Edward Mallinson, kept a tight rein on Scarlet's work schedule and activities.

Mallinson was adamantly opposed to Scarlet's use of *psychometry*—the ability to experience visions from touching a person or an object they had handled—in any official investigation. Unfortunately, his extreme opposition also colored his overall opinion of his assistant surgeon. So any hunch or hint of intuition on Scarlet's part tended to be treated by Mallinson in the same way: by denying Scarlet's ability to act upon it.

By now, in his fifth year on the force, Scarlet expected his boss's resistance to any investigative duties that appeared to be tied to the occult. But he hadn't anticipated the same level of resistance from the Society.

The Society for Psychic and Supernatural Research was a private gentlemen's club, with only thirteen members, that had been formed two years earlier. Its interest was in paranormal, supernatural, or other unusual phenomena that came to its attention. The Society could then investigate, and perhaps (this still wasn't decided yet) publish papers on the events. The gentlemen involved—all men of the world—had decided that a medical doctor with psychic abilities (they knew through discreet channels about Dr. Scarlet's talent), and Django Pierce-Jones, an adept medium who could connect with the spirit world, were prospects that were simply too good to pass up.

Because of his unique ability, Will Scarlet had become the hands-on investigator in the two cases* the Society had studied so far. And with his own unique talents in séances, Pierce-Jones was designated as his fellow sleuth.

The founders of the Society were not concerned with the fashions in magic and mesmerism currently in vogue. They *were* interested in verifiable psychic phenomena in the world around them. If that uncovered paths that led to the supernatural, well, they would follow those paths. They were amateurs in the best sense of the word, and they possessed the zeal of that class—particularly as it revealed itself in privately well-funded clubs and institutions of the time.

But now, the Society seemed determined to apply the brakes to Scarlet's investigation of Max von Leiden. John Borland, Earl of Caversham and a member of Parliament as well as the Society, had spoken to Scarlet about it over lunch recently.

"Things are getting rather too hot, old fellow," as Borland had put it. "There's an extraordinary level of interest—a frenzy really—in this von Leiden chap and the deaths of his rival and this girl who was supposedly his mistress. Any digging from you into that morass

---

* See the first two books in the Dr. Scarlet Mystery series, *Red Season*, and *Year of the Rippers*, both published by Cedar & Maitland Press.

would almost certainly mean that the Society would be dragged into the mud. And then there's this awful disease, or whatever it should be called, that has broken out. Oliver Wyatt's death has been an absolute bonanza for the press. You don't want to stir the pot too vigorously, old fellow. Would you consider backing off for the sake of the good names of the Society's members?"

Scarlet had told MP Borland that he would not consider it.

He didn't know if he was more shocked or angry. Obviously, Max von Leiden had friends in the government, or the request would not have been made at all. And despite Oliver Wyatt's outrageous lifestyle, it was reasonable to assume that he had them too.

Scarlet didn't consider himself a political person, and he frankly had no intention of playing that game. He simply wasn't going to halt his efforts of looking into von Leiden. At the same time, he would continue research into solving the mystery of "this awful disease," The Methuselah Plague.

Unfortunately, none of Scotland Yard's resources—nor, apparently, the Society's—would be at his disposal to succeed at one or the other.

And he didn't have 969 years to do it in, either.

CHAPTER 14

A Question of Magic

ax von Leiden appeared to like the heat.

Once he became aware that Scotland Yard's surgeon-detective was "stirring the pot" (as Borland had put it) where he was concerned, he actually welcomed Scarlet's scrutiny. Scarlet didn't know that at first, but he was soon to find out.

He realized that he couldn't openly confront von Leiden, however—or even get close to him—until he knew more about the man. And so he contacted Horace Bilby once more. Though The Reader's private and exclusive firm specialized in research on British individuals and institutions, the little man informed Scarlet that he was perfectly willing to compile a dossier on the German magician.

Von Leiden was anything but clandestine in the way he lived. Surprisingly, however, there appeared to be little existing documentation on him before he became famous. He was born in Marburg—the Hessen town where the Brothers Grimm had collected their stories—thirty-eight years earlier. The birth certificate (*Geburtsurkunde*) on file, however, had been prepared recently. Likewise, any school records on Maximilian von Leiden were nonexistent. Bilby wasn't able to provide an explanation for this, except to say that the German authorities had pleaded ignorance concerning the absence of records in the civil registration office or Standesamt.

Similarly, it was not known if von Leiden had attended university. And if he had served as a conscript in the Franco-Prussian War of 1870-71, there was no record of that either.

Apparently the first time his name showed up anywhere was as a nineteen-year-old journeyman magician working in carnivals and sideshows on the continent. He was already "Max" von Leiden by then, though not yet The Master of Illusion. The scant newspaper clippings from local papers of this period occasionally mention an up-and-coming magician who demonstrated wild enthusiasm for his art, and stood out because of it. Appearances in marketplaces followed, and then the change necessary for any serious magus: the bookings on the German magic circuit. Now he could perform indoors, where far more sophisticated illusions could be accomplished.

In von Leiden's case, he became known for stage demonstrations that were nearly as reckless as they were spectacular. One thing that made his act attractive—as it always will to the morbidly curious— was the danger inherent in his illusions. Von Leiden never performed The Bullet Catch; but there were other tricks that skirted the boundary of entertainment and tragedy. It was at this time that 'The Master of Illusion' was born.

And there were scandals, as well as occasions where the young magician had to leave town. Gossip preceded and followed von Leiden as he moved around the circuit. The stories one heard were true (mostly): of abused back-stage workers; of young female assistants who suddenly disappeared from the act; of tavern fights with local toughs whom the magician seemed to go out of his way to antagonize. Of course, with each rumour or close escape from arrest, the bigger the house was for the next engagement.

Then, suddenly, von Leiden disappeared, and all his bookings were canceled. For an entire year he wasn't seen on the magic circuit or anywhere else. When he returned, it was with all-new and more spectacular tricks. A few more years of notoriety and success followed, and then came a *two-year* absence. The pattern repeated itself once more—this time for three whole years—before The Master of Illusion returned to the stage in 1887, two years ago.

With each disappearance and return, the illusions became more amazing and inexplicable. The annual tour of *Phantasmagoria*—his new name for his show—was a triumph. Max von Leiden was at the height of his profession, a conjurer arguably without equal. By now he had invented what was possibly the most puzzling illusion in the history of magic: 'Your Fondest Wish.'

This was the enigma known as Max von Leiden.

SCARLET BEGAN HIS INVESTIGATION with a second visit to J.N. Maskelyne at Egyptian Hall.

He realized that if von Leiden were in fact complicit in Giuseppe Caliosto's death, he, Scarlet, needed to know more about the mechanics of The Bullet Catch. It was true that earlier magicians had been killed while performing this dangerous trick. But none of them, as far as Scarlet knew, had been in the midst of a magic war with an archrival.

To demonstrate what he was about to explain, Maskelyne brought out what looked to Scarlet to be a standard military rifle.

"If I'm not mistaken," said Maskelyne, "Caliosto used a firing squad of Ottoman soldiers for his Bullet Catch, didn't he?"

"Yes. I assume that's what they were. They were dressed that way."

"This," said the magician, handing Scarlet the weapon, "is a British Lee-Metford rifle. It's the newly designed standard model for the army, by the way, just adopted this year. The armorer who made this facsimile did a beautiful job don't you think?"

Scarlet was surprised to discover that Maskelyne owned one of the rifles.

"Do you mean to say that you perform The Bullet Catch yourself?"

"Absolutely not. I borrowed this when you told me which trick you were interested in. The Ottoman Army uses a Mauser rifle called the M1887. But the design is very similar to this one, and the audience wouldn't know one way or the other. It's the bolt action we're interested in. When people hear the bolt rammed into place after a bullet is loaded into the gun, it's all very convincing."

"So, the bolt is rigged somehow?"

"Not at all. The bolt hasn't been altered in any way, and the rifle fires normally. That part is real."

At Scarlet's amazed look, Maskelyne explained the nature of the illusion.

"By a sleight of hand—usually a handoff from the assistant to the magician—the conjurer takes possession of the real, marked bullets. The assistant then hands a wax bullet to the person with the weapon—in Caliosto's version of the trick, one to each member of the firing squad.

"While they are loading their weapons, the conjurer uses misdirection to substitute the six real bullets he now has—which he stashes somewhere on his person—with identical-looking ones he has ready. Except that with these bullets, the brass casings have been removed, leaving only the lead or actual projectile. Once the rifles are fired and he shows these lead bullets to the audience, they are pristine, since they haven't been fired at all. To the audience, it looks as though he has intercepted all six bullets in the air, before they've had a chance to pass through any solid objects that would distort them. The wax projectiles loaded into the rifles simply evaporated as each rifle was fired."

"Remarkable."

"And remarkably simple, as I told you before."

"Is that always how the trick is done?"

"Nowadays, it is—or something very similar. Another way to do it is to attach an additional barrel to the rifle, in a way that can't be detected from the house. Then real bullets are loaded into the original barrel. The gun fires a blank from the fake barrel instead of the real barrel, which isn't engaged at all. But there was a very famous case a few years back where that design malfunctioned, and the magician ended up with a bullet in his lung."

"What happened?"

"Carelessness, really. With a setup like that, the gun needs to be thoroughly cleaned of gunpowder residue after each use. This magician got lazy and didn't clean one of the guns properly. One night the build-up of residue ignited, causing the actual barrel with the real bullet to fire."

"My God, how awful."

"The fellow was well known, and it was quite a shock to the profession, I can tell you. His wife, who was his assistant, rushed onstage, but he was already mortally wounded. It was basically the end of that way of performing the trick. That, and an earlier version where everything was real and the shooter simply aimed to slightly miss his target. You can guess how successful that version was."

"And if you wanted to sabotage the trick, how might you do it?"

"Well, it's been done a number of times, so we don't have to guess. Usually, it's some imbecile volunteer who produces his own handgun at the very last moment and shoots the illusionist, evidently to prove a point. Or if he's the one who will be firing the weapon, he loads a real bullet instead of the fake one he's been handed."

"What if it wasn't the audience member doing the sabotaging, but another magician?"

Maskelyne looked closely at Scarlet.

"I see. And is there a magician in particular that you're asking about?"

When Scarlet didn't answer, Maskleyne went on.

"In all fairness to you, Doctor, you should understand that in the history of this profession, there have been many instances where conjurers sabotaged a rival's act. It's usually done by finding out the secret of an illusion, and somehow changing the mechanics of the trick. The rival will find his way backstage during a performance, or bribe a stagehand who is involved in operating the illusion. The goal of these saboteurs is to make the trick go wrong during a performance you see."

"And perhaps to remove one's rival from the scene?"

"If you mean killing him, the answer is no. The aim is to humiliate the rival and cut down on his business. The stakes would be much too high if a hangman's noose followed discovery. Of course, magicians have become injured as a result of these juvenile games."

"But not killed?"

"Not that I've ever heard."

"Until now?"

Maskelyne took the rifle which had been sitting on Scarlet's lap back and returned it to its place in a corner of the room. Sitting back down, he said: "Let's be frank, Dr. Scarlet. You believe that someone deliberately killed Giuseppe Caliosto by sabotaging the trick so that he was shot?"

"Isn't that your opinion of what happened?"

"I really haven't the slightest idea," Maskelyne replied. "I believe you've missed the implications of my earlier explanation of how any sabotage is accomplished, however."

"How do you mean?"

"I said that the aim is usually to discover the secret of how an illusion is accomplished, and then to change the mechanics of it."

"Yes, I remember. And so—?"

"Everyone in my profession knows about The Bullet Catch, and the trick is as old as the hills. The 'secret' of how it's done was explained in a book in 1631! So, no one was about to discover how the illusion was accomplished, and then use that knowledge against the magician performing it. And then there's the question of the mechanics themselves."

"How do you mean?"

"You heard my description of the trick, Doctor. How would anyone have carried out the deception?"

"By substituting real bullets for the ones the assistant handed to the firing squad's members."

"I'm afraid there's a gaping hole in that theory. The assistant had already handed the real bullets to the magician, without the audience noticing, of course. He now has the live cartridges in his possession. His assistant can't give them to the firing squad because she is no longer in possession of them."

"And if she is a confederate, and has an additional six real bullets, previously marked with a red X just the way the volunteer audience member did on stage? And *those* are what she gives to the men with the rifles instead of wax replicas?"

"Another hole, I'm afraid. Marco the Magnificent was standing right next to her. He would easily have noticed that his assistant was giving the soldiers real bullets instead of fake ones. Though they're good enough to fool any eagle-eyed member of the audience, from that close the wax replicas look completely different from actual cartridges. Unless, of course, you're implying that Caliosto knew what was happening and was complicit in his own death."

To Scarlet, this was like arguing a legal point with a lawyer. He couldn't win, and he knew it. Maskelyne must be right about the difficulty—the impossibility?—of someone altering the illusion in a way that would result in Caliosto's death. The damnable difficulty was that The Bullet Catch was too simple an illusion for anyone to be able to monkey with its mechanics.

Which, in one way or another, was what Maskelyne had been telling him all along concerning how stage magic was accomplished.

But Scarlet had also learned another lesson, starting at the age of nine. The truth was that for him and others, the supernatural was just as present as the rest of the world we see around us.

It was 'magic' of an entirely different sort.

Was Max von Leiden practicing it?

CHAPTER 15

An Absolute Darkness

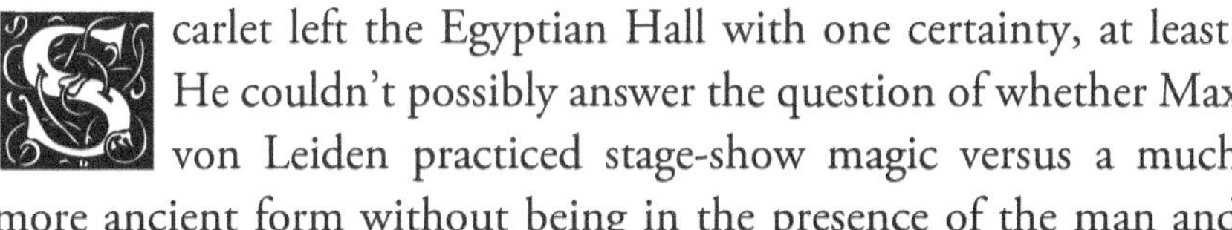carlet left the Egyptian Hall with one certainty, at least. He couldn't possibly answer the question of whether Max von Leiden practiced stage-show magic versus a much more ancient form without being in the presence of the man and scrutinizing him closely.

Leaving the Hall, he'd decided to visit the Queen Victoria Theatre Royal before heading back to Scotland Yard. The theatre was just a mile from Whitehall Place, and the paperwork on his desk could certainly wait.

The time now was 5.40 p.m. It would take less than 15 minutes to get to the Queen Victoria by hansom. So the timing should be perfect: von Leiden would be at the theatre but not yet getting into costume and makeup to go onstage for this evening's performance.

In the cab, he indulged in some fantasizing. He would raise his hand to go on stage the next time von Leiden asked for a volunteer. Standing next to the great magician, he would lean over and whisper:

"I know you murdered Giuseppe Caliosto and drove Frances Murch to suicide."

Von Leiden would stare at him in a moment of shock, the look of cold arrogance and supremacy having vanished from his eyes.

"Come with me quietly after the show, sir, and no one will

guess. The theatre is ringed with my men outside and inside, and you have no hope of escape."

The fantasy bubble—trite dialogue and all—burst when the cab suddenly jolted violently, assaulted by what must be a rather large hole in the road.

———————

THE AREA KNOWN AS *backstage* in a theatre—not the back of the stage itself but the dressing rooms, makeup rooms, costume shop, scene shop, etc.—is usually a maze. The scenic design area, for obvious reasons, is on the same level as the stage. But the rooms where one can find the performers prior to and after curtain is typically one floor below. Anyone unfamiliar with the layout can easily get lost, as there are no signs to tell one where to go. Also, of course, anyone wandering around the area would be questioned as to their business in this part of the building.

Fortunately, Scarlet's Metropolitan Police badge would spare him that kind of trouble. But as it happened, there wasn't any. Everyone was too busy getting from one place to another to pay him any attention. In someone like him not involved with the show, the backstage preparation for *Phantasmagoria* looked like a study in chaos—and not controlled chaos at that. He felt like a boy hiding behind a circus big top, trying not to be trampled by an elephant.

There was a comic moment in one of the corridors. He and von Leiden passed each other; then, as if on cue, both stopped and turned back. The magician was in shirtsleeves with a makeup towel around his neck—and with noticeable grey in his not-yet-blackened temples and goatee.

But it was unmistakably him. The stately pose, the haughtiness, the disdain on the facial features—all of it was impossible to miss at this distance. He waited for Scarlet to walk up to him, not the other way around. But as was appropriate in his domain, he was the first to speak.

"And what do you want, sir? It's obvious you're out of your

element." Then an elegant shrug, with years of stage experience behind it. "Though I suppose your capacity for innocent enjoyment is just as great as any honest man's."

Scarlet responded with a slight, tight grin.

"Excellent, sir . . . a lyric from 'A Policeman's Lot Is Not a Happy One,' from Gilbert and Sullivan's opera *The Pirates of Penzance.*"

A small nod of acknowledgement on von Leiden's part.

"At least you're a man of the theatre. Though I imagine you usually experience it on the other side of the footlights."

"How did you know I was a police officer?"

"My dear Dr. Scarlet, you're wearing a sign that reads, 'I am sniffing around where I don't belong.' Didn't you realize?"

Scarlet found himself looking up at the older and much taller man. He guessed von Leiden's height to be six feet and three inches. He was considering what to say next, when the magician surprised him by extending his hand. Scarlet accepted the gesture, and an iron hand with a hot dry feel to it took possession of his own.

It was a characteristic of Scarlet's psychic power of psychometry that he never knew when it would assert itself. Thankfully, most of the time it didn't. Life would have been unbearable if visions from another's life burst forth whenever he touched that person or an object they had handled. When the visions came, however, they were overpowering, taking complete possession of his mind.

One came now as his hand was locked with von Leiden's.

But it was unlike any psychometric vision he had ever experienced.

What he saw now was . . .

Nothing.

This vision, strangely, *was* no vision. No scenes from von Leiden's life arose in his mind. The psychometric power had surged on in the usual way, but it wasn't producing anything.

What he felt now—he could think of no other way to describe

it—was like a tangible experience of nothingness. It seemed to be an absence of everything: a willful *negation* of it. If he had seen anything, it might have been room after room of blackness leading off in all directions; if he'd heard anything, dead silence. Not the silence of quiet, but a kind of vacuum that pervaded everything because *there never had been sounds.*

It was an absolute darkness that denied the possibility of any light. And it frightened him completely.

Von Leiden let go of his hand, and the world came rushing back.

Time was always skewed during Scarlet's visions. What he experienced seemed to pass by in the actual time it took in real life. But to judge from others' reactions, only a second or two passed, perhaps less. The meant that nearly always, the person whose life he had been experiencing wasn't aware that anything had happened.

He was almost certain that wasn't the case now, however. Von Leiden seemed to be looking straight through him in a way that he didn't like at all.

What had the magician been saying when the psychometric force had hit? Something about Scarlet sniffing around where he didn't belong.

With as much poise as he could muster, he told his antagonist:

"I require a few minutes of your time, sir. I assure you it won't put you behind schedule in terms of preparation for tonight's performance."

"Ah. Naturally, I must bow to your official investigation. Let us go to my dressing room."

It was a surrender born of expediency on von Leiden's part, of course. At any rate, Scarlet didn't correct the other man's mistaken impression concerning how official this investigation was, but simply followed him.

––––––––

THE ORDINARY APPEARANCE OF von Leiden's dressing room

was a complete counterpoint to the mysterious illusions its owner manifested on stage. To Scarlet's eye, it had all the elements of a typical example of the type, except one. The dressing room of a star always contained bouquets of flowers. But there were no flowers in this space.

Von Leiden had walked straight to his makeup-table-and-mirror as soon as they'd entered. Now he sat down and unceremoniously began applying boot-black to his temples and goatee. He leaned close to the glass and worked as carefully as an ingenue getting ready for her first night as a corps dancer in a ballet. He appeared to have forgotten the other man's presence.

Scarlet was sure it was just another of Max von Leiden's subterfuges. For one thing, he was visible in the mirror as he stood behind the makeup table. And for another, he could see the magician's eyes darting up to his reflection every so often, as this absurd illusion of a middle-aged man attempting to look younger continued.

There appeared to be no reason to sneak up on his subject as far as Scarlet could see.

"How well did you know Giuseppe Caliosto?" he said.

Von Leiden replied at once through a mouth stretched tight as he applied blacking to one side of his goatee: "A very dear man, Peppe. And a wonderful conjurer. I warned him against doing The Bullet Catch."

Now the same distortions as the mouth was stretched on the other side: "Such a rare tragedy." A look at Scarlet now in the mirror. "He was only fifty-eight, you know."

"You didn't answer my question."

The magician applied a dab of concealing base under one of his eyes. There was obviously no reason to interrupt the leisurely pace of the cat-and-mouse game.

"Not well . . . and as well as rivals at the top of their profession can know each other. We were friendly, we visited each other's dressing room occasionally, and of course we shared the secrets of illusions. Some illusions, that is."

"And this very public rivalry . . . how real was it behind all the pretense?"

"It was nothing. Naturally, we noticed how many weeks the other was booking into a theatre and how large the crowds were. . . . I'm sorry, Mr. Scarlet, but what does this have to do with the accident that killed Peppe?"

The puzzlement in the voice was excellently done. But Scarlet wasn't having any of it.

"Have you ever sabotaged a rival's trick, Herr von Leiden?"

Now the magician swiveled in his chair so that he was facing Scarlet. He laughed softly and incredulously.

"Well, it's done, of course. Fortunately, it's never happened to me. To answer your question: I've never considered doing anything of the kind. I believe you've seen my act. My illusions are incomparable, and can't be ruined or duplicated. Don't you agree?"

"So, you didn't tamper with Marco the Magnificent's Bullet Catch trick in any way?"

Von Leiden stood and tossed the brush he'd been using to apply his final eye paint onto the makeup table. He removed the towel from around his neck and tossed that on the table as well. Then he turned to Scarlet.

"I did not. Incidentally, I would be very careful in making such an actionable charge, Mr. Scarlet. But of course, you asked it as a question, didn't you?"

With that, he turned his attention to the traditional magician's outfit of black tie and tails hanging on a rack next to the table.

It wasn't a subtle hint. The interview was over.

Scarlet thanked von Leiden for his time and left the room. Miraculously, he found his way to the street without getting lost again.

The interrogation had been both mild and inconclusive. Scarlet had intended the former, and wasn't bothered by the latter.

For one thing, if he had intended to seriously challenge Max von Leiden concerning any complicity in Giuseppe Caliosto's death, he would have used an entirely different line of questioning. For another, he'd have had some evidence in hand before taking that route.

This was simply to put The Master of Illusion on notice.

Call it some misdirection of his own making.

Von Leiden knew now that he was suspected and would be closely watched. It would be an interesting experiment to see if his level of mastery applied to his private life as well, or if in that realm he would begin to make mistakes.

CHAPTER 16

The Robert-Houdin Club

he Robert-Houdin Club is the world's most famous gentlemen's club for magicians. It sits in the heart of London's theatre district on St Martin's Lane, a stone's throw (or in this case, a magic coin's throw) from Leicester Square.

The Club was proposed and immediately voted on at a meeting in 1871 in the Committee Room of the Egyptian Hall. Present at that meeting were four leading magicians and an impresario whose theatres specialized in booking magic acts. The men had gathered for the express purpose of forming a magic society "whose membership will include the best practitioners of the art of magic." The club would "encourage and ensure the propagation of magic as an art form of the highest caliber." It was also hoped that its members would mingle with "men of reputation in a status of equality"—at a time when magicians were often lumped in with actors and actresses as denizens of the lower levels of society.

The occasion for this effort was the death in June of that year at the age of sixty-five of Jean Eugène Robert-Houdin[*]—the most famous magician of the age. It was Robert-Houdin who raised magic

---

[*] Robert-Houdin is pronounced "Ro-bayr Oo-dan." Exactly twenty years later, a boy born as Ehrich Weiss would change his name at the age of seventeen to reflect that of his hero. From then on, he would be known as Harry Houdini.

from a street occupation to the "Soirées Fantastiques" in Paris, and then to the London stages. A watchmaker's son, he had excelled at that profession before beginning to tinker with toys and then more sophisticated mechanical marvels.

One of Robert-Houdin's most famous illusions was The Orange Tree. In this trick, a box with a small tree planted in it would be brought on stage. The magician would ask for a handkerchief from a lady in the audience, which he would immediately make vanish. His next gesture would say to the spectators, "Look at the tree." The small tree would then begin to grow, and slowly produce blossoms which would then fall to the stage one by one. In their place would appear real oranges—one of which would open on its own to reveal the lady's handkerchief inside! Two mechanical butterflies then flew the handkerchief back to its owner in the audience.

The men who met at the Egyptian Hall not only wanted to honor this master illusionist, but had decided that his was the ideal name to adorn their institution. The Robert-Houdin Club had prospered in the eighteen years since its inception. Just as its founders had intended, it was now a London institution frequented not only by conjurers, but respected gentlemen from business, philanthropy, the arts, and government. It was also famous for its library of ancient magical books and scrolls, along with oil paintings of some of history's greatest magicians.

Von Leiden/The Master of Illusion, and J.N. Maskelyne (whose posters promised "Original and Unique Entertainments") were members. Giuseppe Caliosto, the late Marco the Magnificent, had belonged to the club as well. Chung Ling Soo, the Chinese conjuror, was another of the Club's magical stars, presumably because he could relax there in his real American identity of William Ellsworth Robinson.[*]

---

[*] Ironically, Chung Ling Soo was also doomed to die on stage performing The Bullet Catch—which he called Defying the Bullets—because of a mechanical failure in 1918.

A FEW MINUTES AFTER midnight on the 18th of June in our year, a male sifter named Isaac Skelton, who was rummaging through the dust bins and rubbish containers in St Martin's Court, discovered a man's body amid the refuse. After inspecting the pockets and other possible hiding places in the deceased's clothing (there was nothing to be had), Skelton immediately went in search of a Peeler. He found one in the person of police constable Thomas Buckle 234C, who was on his regular Division C beat. 20

The two men hurried to St Martin's Court. Upon questioning by Constable Buckle, Skelton offered his opinion as to the cause of death, which, he assured the policeman, arose solely through a momentary look at the corpse.

"The 'ead's been crushed-in like," said Skelton, frowning. "Not from somethin' fallin' on it, though. Like it exploded inward, if you picture thet."

Despite his hand gestures meant to indicate something round caving in on itself—the policeman thought it all sounded fishy. "'Ere," he said, pulling the fellow closer to smell his breath. But there was no smell of alcohol.

By now they had reached St Martin's Court, and the policeman followed the sifter into the alley. On the ground, amid the dust bins and piles of rubbish heaped up against the back wall of a building, lay the body of a youngish man. He wasn't easy to spot, as his dirty brown jacket and trousers blended in with the trash he was lying in. He looked tall and lanky, and the pants he had on were too short for him by at least a couple of sizes. They revealed skinny white ankles above socks that were, by this stage of their life, of an indeterminate colour.

From a distance that allowed him to avoid disturbing any physical evidence, PC Buckle shone his Bull's Eye lantern on the body and the area around it. He was looking for any external signs of violence or injury, as well as any objects that might have been left behind by an assailant (there were none). Behind him, he could feel the old man bending forward to get a view of his own. Once the officer had satisfied himself that there was no discernible evidence on the ground, he stepped closer to the body. Very carefully, he shifted what looked like the remains of a box with thin wooden slats that had been broken when the dead man fell into his current position. Now he could see the head more clearly.

"Crikey," Buckle said softly. Just over his right shoulder, he heard Skelton draw in his breath sharply.

"I'll be batty-fanged," said the old man. "It's jus' as I told yer, idn't it? He don't hardly have no head left, least not that looks like one. What erya reckon happened?"

"Damfino,*" replied Buckle, slipping momentary back into the language of his own less-than-upper-class upbringing. He wasn't really paying attention to the question anyway. He was trying to make sense of what he was seeing on the ground in front of him.

For one thing, the face looking up at him was all wrong. The features were all there; but they were rearranged in a crazy-quilt pattern worse than Frankenstein's monster, with nothing but the right eye in its proper location.

Then the thought came to PC Buckle that the problem lay in the *skull*, not the face. The features staring back at him were crazily distorted, that was true. But in terms of any medical knowledge, as a layman he had to agree with Mr. Skelton: the skull of this man had been compressed so severely that the landscape of the face was hardly recognizable as human.

The skull must have been severely *squeezed* somehow—and more from the right side as one looked at it. It was as though a right-handed giant or someone of supernatural strength had taken the head in his hands and pressed relentlessly. The mind of the constable dismissed the silly thought and sought purchase on a question that

---

* Damned if I know.

made sense: what might have applied such pressure to this man's head to distort it in this way?

Whatever caused it, the compression must have been most severe at the man's left temple. The skull had caved in so completely on that side that the upper teeth and jaw now lay higher than normal and occupying the space where the bones of the temple had been, pressed up against the left ear. The lower teeth and jaw had been forced in the opposite direction—downward and far to the right. The mouth now gaped wide because of this radical rearrangement of both jaws. In fact, the face appeared to have grown an entirely new skull plate on the right side, where the lower jaw had finally stopped its sideways movement.

The left eye had disappeared completely as the facial structure had collapsed. The eye and its orbit appeared to lie somewhere at the bottom of what looked like a mine cave-in of cheek and eye socket on the left side. A large dent in the forehead was visible just above this region, and Buckle had an idea that there was probably a sizable hole underneath the skin where the skull plates had separated in that area.

He tried to imagine how long the force that had crushed this man's head had lasted, and what it must have felt like to the victim. But the thought was too upsetting, and he let it go.

He wondered instead if there was similar damage to the man's neck that might have occurred as his head was pressed or wrenched, not visible now because of the clothing. He didn't want to poke around any closer to the corpse to see if there was, though. Suppose his bleedin' head fell off!

The detectives, or at least the sergeant, could deal with it. He straightened up and began blowing his whistle vigorously.

ST MARTIN'S COURT, WHERE the body was found, was a scruffy thoroughfare just two blocks long. It functioned mostly as a shortcut between Charing Cross Road and St Martin's Lane in the Theatre

District. It was the home of one modest theatre specializing in variety acts, many small shops, and only one building of distinction—and even that was officially located on St Martin's Lane, at the corner where the Court met the Lane.

That was 75-78 St Martin's Lane: the address of the Robert-Houdin Club.

Had it not been for that fact, Scarlet would not have known of a possible link between the magician's club and the body discovered just around the corner from it. Not yet, at least.

He was looking through the Post Mortem and Case Book, a daily requirement of his job, when he came across the John Doe report of the dead man in St Martin's court. The case was certainly an interesting one due to the crushed skull, an unusual manner of death to say the least. But his eye was caught by the location where the body was found. His colleague Dr. Dickinson had written in his case notes that the victim was discovered "around the corner from the magician's club."

Dickinson's post-mortem itself was a painstaking description and measurements of skull plates and their displacements, the numerous and severe fractures present, and the radical transfiguration of the facial structure due to these deficits. Scarlet could only imagine how long all of this took his colleague to measure and record. And then, of course, the rest of the autopsy had had to be completed, no matter how obvious the cause of death seemed.

For some years now, a raging argument had been ongoing in medical circles and published papers on whether the practice of autopsy was a valuable scientific tool. To Scarlet, there was no doubt whatsoever: an 1887 survey had demonstrated that forty percent of pre-mortem diagnoses were incorrect as revealed by an autopsy! Clearly, medicine had as much to learn from dead patients as living ones.

A thought came to him suddenly now, and he checked the Chief Surgeon's Assignment Sheet. This was the duty roster in which his superior Dr. Mallinson assigned cases to his staff of assistant chief medical examiners. In questionable or suspicious deaths, it was routine procedure to assign a surgeon-detective to coordinate with the detective branch or the special unit within that branch, the Criminal Investigation Department (CID).

Scarlet saw that he had been assigned to this case.

He was certain that it was sheer coincidence. Mallinson would have had no knowledge of his interest in magic.

Or in a magician who went by the stage name of The Master of Illusion.

CHAPTER 17

St Michael and All the Angels

 search of the doss houses, or common lodging houses, in the nearby police divisions soon uncovered the decedent's identity. He was twenty-five-year-old John Roach from Berkshire, the county directly to the west of London.

Until two years ago when he'd come to London, Roach had been an assistant custodian at a church in the village of Lambourn, Berks. No one knew much about him here in the city, apart from the fact that he was poor, and as one pub owner had described him: "a common scammer, half-rats most of the time." By that was meant the men and women—many of them habitually half-drunk—who will scam in any way they can to pay for a doss house bed when they can afford it, and sleep in alleyways or the dark corners of courtyards when they can't.

Roach was known to elevate himself to actual drunkenness whenever he had the 3 ½ pence for a pint of beer. That was almost exactly the 4d. that a bed for the night at a doss house cost. Like others, though, Roach frequently chose the beer over the bed. The word on the street was that he could be belligerent when drunk, and was generally suspicious of everyone. When he'd had a bit of luck— or more likely, had nicked the purse of a gentlemen passed out from drink—he would immediately spend it on some quick intimacy up against a wall in an alley. All of this made him so similar to the other men who lived one step up from the gutter as to make him virtually invisible.

Poor John Roach! The cost of things was even factored into investigating his death. The Yard's resources—like all of Her Majesty's offices—were limited. In most cases, they simply couldn't be expended in investigations where there wasn't an obvious need to do so, or in cases that lacked social prominence.

On the other hand, the case of the man with the crushed skull *had been* played up enough in the press so as to create public interest. And Lambourn *is* only 70 miles from Central London. There was also no denying that Berkshire *was* one of the counties specified in the Western Railways Bill of 1835 that had extended the capital's railway network westward.

And so funds were allocated for Scarlet to take the Great Western Railway from Paddington Station to the village of Lambourn in Berkshire.

LAMBOURN WAS FAMOUS FOR two things: (1) horse racing, and (2) the Seven Barrows, where one could find thirty burial mounds dating back to 4,000 B.C.

The village, located in an area sometimes known as "The Valley of the Race Horse," was the second largest center for racehorse training in the United Kingdom (after Newmarket in Suffolk). It offered a rehabilitation clinic for jockeys with injuries, and even boasted an equine hospital. If any Bronze Age individuals had emerged from those burial mounds and were walking about in the village, though, nobody told Scarlet about it.

His destination was St Michael and All the Angels Church. The church site was at the intersection of two main roads where the Saxons had worshipped and which, one hundred and fourteen years after the Norman Conquest, became the site for the church's construction in 1180 A.D. The building (as a brochure informed Scarlet) had been added onto and reconfigured during a number of centuries since then. But from the outside—at least to Scarlet—it looked like every other Norman church in England, boasting a square bell tower with four small pillars on the top.

The interior of the ancient church, surprisingly, was filled with light, due to the white stone used and the natural light filtering through the arched windows located atop the high curved arches above the nave. The wood used in the pews and floor was also aged, dark and rustic. It added to the simple unadorned beauty of the place.

Scarlet expected the current vicar to reflect these surroundings, like someone cast for the part. He'd be slightly massive, with flowing grey hair above and surrounding his Church of England collar. He would possess the air of someone who'd just removed his battle armor (now that the pesky Saxons had been conquered) to tend to the too-long neglected spiritual side of things.

The reality was considerably different. The person who met him was small and slight, with prematurely white hair cut neatly around a youngish face. He had a thin pointed nose, a wide mouth, and calm grey eyes. He was smiling as he walked up the church's center aisle to greet Scarlet, his hand extended.

"I'm sorry I wasn't clearer," the Rev. Michael Whipham said as he shook his visitor's hand. "I was expecting you in my office, which is back and to the right. Fortunately, our church echoes wonderfully, so I heard your footsteps. Did you have a pleasant journey?"

"I did, thank you . . . should I call you 'Father'? How may I address you?"

"You're very wise to ask, Doctor Scarlet. In the marketplace, I would say, 'Sir' would be appropriate. But here, please call me Michael."

"I will. I wasn't sure whether 'Rev. Whipham' would be appropriate."

"Goodness, no. People don't realize that 'Reverend' is an adjective. You wouldn't say, for instance, 'Nice sermon, Intelligent,' would you?"

"Perhaps I would, if the person giving it was."

"Well, you have me there," came the reply, and both men laughed.

"We'll sit here, if you don't mind," the priest said, indicating the nearest pew. When they were seated, he made an apologetic gesture. "Church pews aren't meant to be comfortable, I'm afraid. They're God's reminder that He didn't intend to make life easy for us."

"It's a beautiful church. Thank you for agreeing to see me."

"To tell you the truth, it's a bit of excitement to see a new face in the village. How can I help you?"

"I'm investigating the recent death of John Roach, who I understand was an assistant custodian here at the church."

"Oh, I am sorry to hear that. He was quite a young man, wasn't he?"

"You didn't know him personally, then?"

"No, he left at the same time I was assigned here. Actually, just before my arrival. What happened to him?"

"We're not sure. His skull was crushed. We don't know yet if it was accidental, or something else. So, you can't tell me anything about him?"

"I'm afraid not. You see, I came here two years ago. There was a . . . well, the vicar before me, Charles Hathersley, was murdered. By the time I arrived as his replacement, Mr. Roach had already left the area. I only know about him from people mentioning him in passing, and his pay records, of course. I never met him personally."

"What was the date of Rev. Hathersley's murder?"

"It was shortly before Christmas, last year. The fourteenth of December."

"Was there any suspicion that Roach was involved in the murder?"

"None that I ever heard of. The truth is, Doctor, I doubt whether young John Roach would have been able to do something like that alone."

"What do you mean? How did Charles Hathersley die?"

"He was crucified. Sometime during the early morning of December 14th, a cross was erected just over there, on that wall to the right of the pulpit. The vicar, Mr. Hathersley, was found nailed to it later that morning. He had been dead for some time."

"Jesus. I'm sorry, Father," Scarlet immediately apologized for the profanity.

But The Rev. Michael Whipham shook his head.

"No need, sir. With something this evil, it's understandable."

"Yes, of course."

"I'm afraid you don't know what I mean."

"I'm sorry," said Scarlet, "but I'm a little confused. What *do* you mean?"

"The cross was erected upside down, Doctor."

CHAPTER 18

The Weight of the Evidence

The arrival of the Great Western Railways train at Paddington Station in London took Scarlet by surprise. He had been wrestling with five questions for the entire ride, making him oblivious to the scenery rushing by and the time that was passing.

The questions occupying his mind were these:

* Was John Roach's departure from Lambourn, immediately after the Rev. Hathersley's murder, as suspicious as it seemed?

* Did Roach have anything to do with the vicar's crucifixion?

* Why did the young man leave his steady job and move to London so penniless that he had to stay in flop houses?

* Who would have wanted him dead? (Despite what Scarlet had told Rev. Whipham, there was no evidence whatsoever that Roach had died as the result of an accident.)

* Was the location of the body—around the corner from the Robert-Houdin Club—just a coincidence?

He bought a copy of *The Times* at a newsstand, looking forward to clearing his head of mysteries he couldn't solve at the moment. The following headline and story were in the far-left column on the front page:

PLAGUE DEATHS

NUMBERS MOUNT

HOME SECRETARY MEETS WITH PM

The Secretary of State for the Home Department, Mr. Matthew White Ridley, 2d Viscount Ridley, met with the Prime Minister Lord Salisbury at Whitehall yesterday to discuss the mounting numbers of mysterious deaths in London due to abnormally rapid aging.

Though still limited in terms of numbers, deaths from the so-called Methuselah Plague, whose victims age swiftly and prematurely, continue to mystify health authorities and physicians. The medical condition of unknown origin rose to prominence recently with the death of Oliver Wyatt, well-known society figure and gambling club habitué.

Home Secretary Viscount Ridley was quoted as saying: "We have our best minds on this at the moment. I am told that we are rapidly making progress on what causes this terrible condition, and I hope to have further news for you shortly."

This, Scarlet knew, was rubbish. He wasn't aware of any hospital, doctor, or researcher who was making progress concerning the Methuselah Plague, rapid or otherwise.

The odd thing—not mentioned in any newspaper stories he had seen but known to the Yard's investigators—was that the people falling victim to the disease were in the prime of their lives. Not necessarily regarding age (the victims ranged from their teens into their sixties), but in terms of the prosperity they were experiencing at the time they were struck down. Whether that was due to the fact that health professionals had such a small cohort of patients to study, or was a factor better understood by an economist or historian, he had no idea.

Twenty minutes later, the cab from Paddington Station deposited him at the Yard's headquarters in Whitehall, just three miles away. And it was only a few minutes after that, that Scarlet gave some serious thought to the well-known superstition that bad news comes in threes.

On the lower floor near the autopsy room, he ran into Christopher ("Kit") Dickinson, his colleague who had performed the post-mortem on John Roach. A clearly upset Kit told him that his office had been broken into last night, and the 1889 Post Mortem and Case Book—which had been in Kit's possession so he could write up his notes on the Roach autopsy—had been stolen.

Scarlet made up his mind that he would get through the paperwork waiting on his desk as quickly as possible. His next step in the Roach murder investigation suddenly seemed more urgent.

Even before he sat down at his desk, however, he wrote two short notes, which he handed to a messenger with instructions for delivery. Then he began attending to that paperwork.

FROM SCARLET'S VANTAGE POINT where he stood in the foyer of the Robert-Houdin Club, the place appeared to be a maze of stages, seating areas, and shiny surfaces.

The three rooms he could see from here were similar in design.

Each contained a combination of four-person booths with tables, and comfortable chairs set apart, also with a small table at hand. The booths sat on small step-up stages, and the individual chairs faced slightly larger stages, which were also a single step up from the floor.

Without a doubt, the now-empty club was a place built of magic and for magic. The purpose of the stages seemed obvious: magicians must provide close-up magic acts for people sitting at the tables or in the booths. The setup would allow conjurers to move from stage to stage so that everyone would get a brief private show.

In the corners of all three rooms stood museum-like displays filled with paraphernalia of magic acts of the past. In some of them dummies—or perhaps they were wax figures—were dressed in the stage costumes the magicians who performed these acts must have worn. Black and red were the dominant colors everywhere: on the walls, in the upholstery of the booths, and even on the ceilings.

Scarlet turned around to see a Club official standing in front of him with a look of professional politeness on his face. Where in the world had the fellow come from? Perhaps he'd just stepped out of one of these displays. Or was it all done with magic?

"May I help you, sir?"

Scarlet identified himself and mentioned his appointments at the Club.

"Ah, yes, Dr. Scarlet. If you would come this way . . ."

A golden door marked MEMBERS ONLY led to an entirely different world. This was obviously one of the private rooms at the Club, where the magicians could relax and enjoy the privileges of their status in the profession.

The enormous room had an oriental rug on the floor which was larger than any Scarlet had ever seen. The wing chairs were of comfortable-looking dark brown leather, the tables of similarly dark polished wood. The fireplace mantel was constructed of a material that looked like ivory, and the crystal chandelier overhead must have held fifty lit candles. The walls were a pleasant shade between sea and sage green, and were adorned with stately-looking portraits of magicians from earlier eras. The frames were of many different sizes and shapes, but all were painted gold.

Seated at the largest table in the center of the room were five men, all of whom stood when the Club official announced Scarlet. One of them—Scarlet wasn't surprised to see—was Max von Leiden.

He had sent two separate notes: one to the Club's officers, and the other to von Leiden. It wasn't necessary that every one of the officers Scarlet had written to would be at the Club at the time he specified, and the group gathered here seemed sufficient. They would have the information he was looking for: the Club's official position regarding John Roach's death.

His note to Herr von Leiden had been less polite and more official. He had written that he had additional questions following their initial meeting. He would appreciate The Master of Illusion meeting him at the Club where he had an appointment to speak to the management.

He didn't care that von Leiden would resent more questioning, for the simple reason that he had no intention of making things easy for the magician. He also wanted the interrogation to be away from von Leiden's turf at the theatre, and in the presence of witnesses.

Each man now introduced himself as they stood around the table. There was no shaking of hands. Scarlet declined the offer of anything to drink, and with that the fellow who'd brought him to the room departed and everyone sat down.

"How may we be of service to you, Mr. Scarlet?" asked the gentleman who had just introduced himself as the Club's secretary.

Jonathan Bright was a robust fellow in a handsome brown checkered suit with a heavy watch chain, looking for all the world like he should be some organization's secretary. Scarlet wondered if he had been a magician himself, or if the Robert-Houdin Club subscribed to the new tradition of hiring a professional man to oversee the group's affairs, whether he was in that line of business or not.

Scarlet thought that Secretary Bright's manner was just what it should be. He gave the impression that the Club was completely open to police inquiry at any time; but won't you, dear chap, be brief in your business so we can get back to important affairs.

The Metropolitan Police's detectives had questioned the Club's leadership and anyone present at the establishment when Roach's body was discovered, of course. But that had been before Scarlet's trip to Lambourn and the information he had obtained there. So far, the Yard hadn't uncovered any evidence that told them what Roach was doing in St Martin's Court—just around the corner from the Club—at the time of his death. The first question in today's visit, therefore, was obvious.

"Can you tell me if you recognize this man?" Scarlet asked, handing to the fellow nearest him a photograph of John Roach. The Rev. Whipham had kindly let him borrow the photograph from the employment files at St Michael and All the Angels Church in Lambourn. A post-mortem photo of a man with a crushed head certainly wouldn't have been of any use.

"Was he here at the Club on the night of June 17th, or have you seen him on the premises at any other time?"

Each of the men shook his head when he saw the photo.

"I see. I'll be asking each of your employees the same question in a moment, as I said in my note," added Scarlet.

"You're perfectly welcome to do so, of course, Dr. Scarlet," said an elderly man with unruly white hair parted in the middle. He was tall; and he might once have been heavier, for his clothes looked to be a size or two too large. "But the four of us at this table—excepting Herr von Leiden, of course, who is busy performing—are here at the Club virtually all the time. We're extremely familiar with our clientele who are, after all, nearly all magicians themselves. If this fellow came here, I think we'd have noticed."

Scarlet could well believe it. The man—who was incongruously named, if he remembered correctly, Mr. Young—had the look of someone who had nothing better to do in his declining years than busy himself around the insides of a private club, irritating everyone.

"And was there anyone else at the Club that night that any of you noticed particularly? Someone unknown to you? Or were any of the regulars acting out of character?"

Everyone at the table shook their heads except von Leiden. Scarlet looked at him expectantly.

"I am a magician, sir," von Leiden told him. "And these gentlemen watch magic acts every evening here at the Club. I can assure you that if anything out of the ordinary happened on that night, or any other, we would have made note of it."

"And you didn't, Herr von Leiden? Notice it or make a note of it, I mean."

"I hadn't finished, sir. I was about to say that we would already have discussed it among ourselves. Given the unfortunate events on the night in question, we would of course have contacted the authorities immediately and shared any information we had with them."

"Well, we're grateful for your cooperation," said Scarlet briskly. "If I may interview your employees now?"

But von Leiden evidently couldn't let sleeping dogs lie.

"You will excuse me, gentlemen," he began, flicking his gaze at the others and then settling it on Scarlet. "I'm afraid my schedule won't permit me to be available for any further questioning. This is the second time Dr. Scarlet has specifically sought me out in that regard. There won't be a third."

Breeding and protocol allowed the men at the table to avoid displaying any emotion at this statement. But their shocked silence was just as eloquent.

"Are you refusing official questioning by the Metropolitan Police, Herr von Leiden?"

"I am saying that any investigation carried out with repeated visits to the same individuals and without sufficient purpose, is . . . unwelcome."

Scarlet said nothing, and in the strained silence Secretary Bright spoke up.

"We will have the employees brought in now, Doctor."

"Thank you," replied Scarlet. "One at a time, of course."

The staff of the Robert-Houdin Club professed as much ignorance as the management as to anything unusual occurring on the night of John Roach's death. When Scarlet was finished with his questions, the Club's officers escorted him through the main entrance to the front steps.

And then an extraordinary thing happened.

Two carriages were waiting in front of the Club on St Martin's Lane. One was the hansom cab Scarlet had flagged down at Whitehall, and whose driver waited for him now as instructed. The other was von Leiden's much larger—and considerably more expensive—ebony-painted landau, drawn by two large black Hackney horses with braided manes.

As Scarlet and the Club's officers emerged through the front door, someone screamed. Looking toward the sound, Scarlet saw a young woman standing stock-still in the middle of the street. She was dressed in typical nanny fashion in a black dress and white overgarment. Behind her stood a pram, unattended. The girl was frozen in mid-gesture: one hand halted in the air near her mouth and her eyes opened wide.

Running away from her at full speed was a tow-headed boy, no more than three years old. He seemed hell-bent on escape, his blond head angled down and forward as his arms pumped and his legs pushed for all they were worth. He was headed straight for the two carriages.

Von Leiden's landau was parked in front of the hansom cab, as he had arrived at the Club before Scarlet. The nanny screamed again—"No! No!"—choosing not the boy's name but instead trying to halt the imminent danger she had just noticed from occurring. For the horses hitched to the landau, the two big Hackneys, had noticed the boy.

They both turned their heads toward him; and it must have frightened the lad, for he stopped dead in his tracks, looked up at the huge animals and yelled. The horses shied and reared up on their hind legs, pushing the carriage back and spilling the driver onto the pavement. The boy, who must have been scared out of his wits, ran in the wrong direction, disappearing under the three black shapes of the pair of horses and the carriage.

Then the world—which seemed to have been holding its breath—breathed again, as people began rushing toward the carriage from all angles. Scarlet had been closest to the landau on the Club's steps, and was the first to reach it.

"Make way, I'm a doctor!" he shouted.

He bent low. Now he could see the boy. The child was lying on his back under the rear portion of the landau, looking more shocked than scared. The animals were both snorting nervously and stepping back and forth, so that the carriage rolled a little each way each time they moved.

The boy's left foot was pinned to the pavement by the landau's large rear left wheel. No, not his foot, Scarlet saw now—his *shoe*. Incredibly, the boy's shoe must have slipped partly off, so when the wheel rolled over it, it pinned the leather of the shoe to the ground, not the foot inside it. But if the horses moved backward any more, the wheel would follow suit and crush the boy's foot and ankle.

Scarlet remained as still as he could. He didn't dare stand up, for the movement might spook the horses.

"Don't move," he heard a deep voice say behind him.

Then Max von Leiden came into his field of vision on his right, stepping swiftly but silently past him to get to the wheel. There, he breathed in deeply and bent his knees, keeping his back straight. He grasped two spokes of the carriage wheel, at 4 and 8 o'clock on a clock's face. Then he began lifting.

His own face became congested, turning dark red. Fifteen seconds . . . twenty; and Scarlet, still crouching as he watched, thought von Leiden would begin to bleed from the nose any second now from a burst blood vessel. But no blood escaped that reddened face. From this close, Scarlet heard the wagon's springs begin to creak. Then the landau rose an inch . . two inches, beginning now to tilt slightly the other way.

And now the boy quickly yanked his foot—which must have been compressed tightly in the shoe—to safety. He had just cleared the wheel; for when von Leiden eased the carriage down and the wheel came to rest once again on the misshapen shoe and the end of a stocking now peeking out of it, the boy's bare toes were not more than two inches away.

The lad had begun to wail, but the nanny already had him in the inescapable grip (this time) of her embrace. Watching the two of them, Scarlet hardly noticed von Leiden open the landau's door and step inside. And he didn't notice at all that the driver was back in his seat until the carriage began moving and he automatically stepped out of the way.

He wasn't wondering about this uncharacteristic act of charity on Max von Leiden's part.

He was thinking instead of the man's strength.

———

WHEN HE ARRIVED HOME forty-five minutes later, he wrote one more note.

This one was to Horace Bilby.

CHAPTER 19

Spectacular Ghosts

he next day, June the 22nd, posters began appearing around the city, announcing a final gala night for The Master of Illusion's *Phantasmagoria* magic show. Von Leiden's run at the Queen Victoria Theatre Royal had been extended once more, this time until Saturday, July 6th.

The advertisements advised that the final performance on that date would *absolutely conclude the London appearances of this world-famous conjurer.* But that wasn't the wording that caught the public's eye. There was also this "explanation," printed in large bold type near the top of the bills, placards, and sandwich boards that were appearing around London:

THE ILLUSION OF THE AGE! —
THE FINAL PERFORMANCE IN LONDON!

SPECIAL EXPLANATION TO THE PUBLIC

Herr von Leiden wishes it understood that he will present to theatregoers, FOR THAT NIGHT ONLY, a spectacular "Procession"—featuring ALL of this season's participants in the "Your Fondest Wish" experiment.

There will be no interval or intermission at the final performance, and no one will be admitted to the theatre after the curtain goes up.

No allowance made for any ticket not used.

CHAPTER 20

A Marker At Last

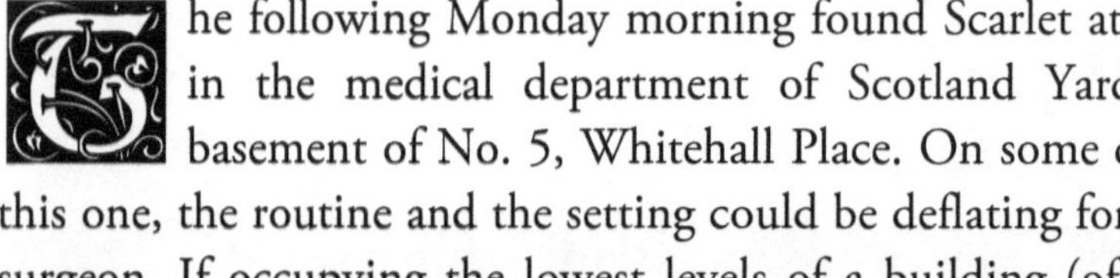he following Monday morning found Scarlet at his desk in the medical department of Scotland Yard in the basement of No. 5, Whitehall Place. On some days, like this one, the routine and the setting could be deflating for a police surgeon. If occupying the lowest levels of a building (offices and examination rooms in the basement, morgue in the sub-basement) weren't enough to lower your opinion of yourself, there was also the inescapable reality that you were surrounded by an endless procession of death.

At the moment, Scarlet had three such deaths on his mind.

Giuseppe Caliosto—Marco the Magnificent—purportedly killed by accident during The Bullet Catch illusion.

Frances Murch, the young apprentice magician who had died a suicide.

John Roach, the former assistant church custodian from Lambourn who'd had his head crushed in St Martin's Court here in London.

At this stage, Scotland Yard's investigation into Caliosto's death was perfunctory at best. The Yard couldn't justify much in the way of time and man-hours on the death of a magician who'd expired during a dangerous magic trick. And it was simply uninterested in an all-too-common suicide of a young girl who was almost certainly disappointed in love. Only Scarlet believed that Max von Leiden was the shared link in these two deaths.

As to the Roach murder, it was the only one of the three cases that was part of an active investigation. The Yard had finally classified the case as homicide, having no other explanation for a man dying from a crushed skull in that time and place. The possibility that Herr von Leiden was involved in this case as well had been only another hunch on Scarlet's part.

Until four days ago and his visit to Lambourn.

He could do nothing more now, however, except wait. The information coming from Horace Bilby would tell him whether the clue he'd picked up last Friday was part of a real fire, or just smoke without a source.

———————

HE PICKED UP THE memorandum from Sir Edward Mallinson, Chief Surgeon of the Metropolitan Police, which had been sitting on his desk when he arrived at his office this morning and read it again. It stated:

TO ASSISTANT CHIEF SURGEON RANK AND ABOVE:

You will please direct your attention that is not otherwise engaged, which is to say in active investigations or clinical duties, e.g., autopsies and laboratory results, to conduct relevant research into the recent deaths from the public health emergency known as The Methuselah Plague. (The man wouldn't know a full-stop if one bit him on the nose!) Relevant records and information heretofore gathered on this condition can be found in the MPO Records section.

All London hospitals currently conducting research on same have been directed by this Office to supply MPO with relevant information at the earliest. You may also contact any of the hospitals directly. You are hereby directed to supply this Office with any new data* shared with you by these institutions not currently in the Records section.

* Please use this term when referring to numerical facts compiled for current or future reference. See my memorandum of 21 April 1897.

Scarlet was convinced he already had the information he needed on the Plague. If one of the hospitals had had a breakthrough in uncovering the etiology of the disease, his department would already know about it—and the press wouldn't have been far behind. But to his knowledge, there hadn't been any new developments on the medical side.

He believed that the best way to quickly gain new insights into the rapid aging condition lay in the population affected. Breakthroughs at the major organ or cellular levels might be decades away.

As he thought more along these lines, he realized he welcomed the time it was taking for Bilby to report back to him. He needed something to clear his head concerning the Caliosto, Murch, and Roach deaths and Max von Leiden's possible connection to them, and focusing on the health emergency would accomplish that.

For once, therefore, a memo from Mallinson wasn't unwelcome.

Would wonders never cease?

He placed the file with his Plague notes in the center of the desktop.

––––––––

HE EXAMINED THE FIGURES on the sheet of paper he was holding.

They showed an anomaly. Over the past month, the number of deaths from the Plague had inched up slowly but steadily in the

U.K., but had ceased in the other countries involved: France, Germany, and the United States. In fact, it had been some months since a death due to the disease was noted abroad.

And the population affected by the condition remained too low. Based on governmental records of people whose deaths could now be attributed to The Methuselah Plague, over the past two years, seventy-four individuals in the United Kingdom of Great Britain and Ireland had died, and a little over two hundred worldwide.

If this was a communicable contagion, the numbers should be much higher, and they would rapidly have followed a familiar curve or spike upwards. Likewise, a genetic source of the disease couldn't be the answer. If that were the case, the population affected would be much more sharply defined geographically. And of course, the condition would have shown itself much earlier in human development than to suddenly rear its head now.

The limited scope of the Plague, on the other hand was an advantage. It meant that anyone studying the rapid aging disease could look at all the data (Mallinson loved the newly coined word, and Scarlet had to admit it did serve a purpose) at once.

For instance, there weren't thousands of cases for researchers to look at in this country, but only a few dozen. In fact, Scarlet was holding a list of those names in his hands right now. The number was roughly equal of people who had died in the provinces versus those who developed the condition and expired in London.

He recognized two of the London names, of course, for both had been his patients: Mrs. Walter Keeley-Campbell, and Oliver Wyatt. He had seen Mrs. Keeley-Campbell in his surgery on April 5th: a forty-six-year-old woman who looked three decades older. According to the information in the list he was holding, she had died in early June, or four months after the date she gave Scarlet as the start of her symptoms.

Oliver Wyatt had actually died during his examination in Scarlet's surgery on May 31st. He had been just twenty-four years old, and he had told Scarlet that his symptoms had begun in January of that year. Again, his death had come four months after the condition first began to show itself.

By now, anyone researching the disease had seen the same progression in every patient: emergence of symptoms, accelerated aging beginning immediately thereafter, and rapid physical decline followed by death within 16-18 weeks.

Yet to date, no one had uncovered any evidence of a biological agent responsible. There was only the senescence itself, which was a symptom and not a cause.

By necessity, then, Scarlet had begun thinking along different lines. Why not concentrate on the population instead of a disease vector? The idea had been trying to make itself heard in Scarlet's mind for some time, and now he was ready to listen to it.

He told himself to think like a practitioner of the newest branch of medicine, not yet thirty years old, known as epidemiology. "Epidemiologists," as they were beginning to be called, focused on the incidence and control of disease in a population.

Looking at the problem from that point of view made the key question this one: Was there anything in this list that represented a common denominator from a societal standpoint?

If anything, thinking that way seemed to make things harder. These names were a perfect cross section of London society, ranging across ages, occupations, dwelling places, and social standing. The ages of the victims (before the rapid aging overtook each of them), seemed irrelevant as well, ranging from eighteen to sixty-nine. Without exhaustive detective work and interviewing of the relatives of these people, it seemed unlikely that a common thread could be discerned. And of course, the medical department of the Yard had nothing like the resources needed for that kind of investigation.

But there had to be something here among the names!

There was also the maddening thought that there *was* something, staring him right in the face but that he simply wasn't seeing.

"Not with these eyes," he told himself after two hours of going over the list again and taking notes. It was time to take a break.

Amid the papers fouling his desktop (as Scarlet usually thought of departmental correspondence), was something he hadn't noticed before. It was a note from Pierce-Jones, written on his friend's personalized stationery a day earlier. It read:

Von Leiden's Phantasmagoria is giving a final gala performance on Sat., 6 July before the show leaves London. There will be some kind of spectacular performance of "Your Fondest Wish." I've booked rather good seats for the two of us. Tra-la!
Regards
Django

He tossed the note onto the desktop and left his office to get a cup of tea from the canteen. But part of the way there, he slowed his pace, and then stopped. A thought was tapping softly in the depths of his subconsciousness. He stayed still and let it make its way up to his conscious mind. Once it did, he walked quickly back to his office, put his frock coat back on over his waistcoat, and prepared to leave the building.

He had an idea that the Robert-Houdin Club would have what he needed somewhere in their records.

CHAPTER 21

The Man Who Rode the Railway

n the doorway of his office, however, he nearly collided with a messenger trying to enter it. The lad and Scarlet both apologized. But he noticed the return address on the packet the messenger was holding and his mind refocused immediately.

It was from Bilby.

He gave the boy his tip, placed the brown-paper-wrapped package on his desk, and took off the frockcoat he'd put on not a minute earlier. Then he sat down at his desk, picked up a pair of scissors, and pulled the parcel toward him by its string.

Before him now on the desktop was an itinerary of *Phantasmagoria* in its English tour of the last three months of the previous year and the beginning of this year. Bilby had also included the show's international bookings prior to this period, even though Scarlet had told him to ignore them.

This is what the report on the U.K. tour showed:

The Master of Illusion's *Phantasmagoria* U.K. Tour

October 1888 – January 1889

City	Dates
Birmingham	October 13 – November 10, 1888
Oxford	November 17 – December 1
Swindon	December 8 – 15
Portsmouth	December 22 – 29
Brighton	January 5 – 19, 1889
London	January 26 – London engagement begins.

Every *Phantasmagoria* booking began and ended with a Saturday evening performance. But it was a specific date and location that Scarlet was interested in. He found his notes from his interview with the Rev. Michael Whipham at St Michael and All the Angels Church in Lambourn.

He was sure he remembered the date correctly, but he double-checked now.

Yes: The Rev. Charles Hathersley had been found crucified on an inverted cross on the morning of December 14, 1888.

It was a simple matter now to calculate the distance between Swindon, Wiltshire, where the show was performing on that date, and Lambourn, Berkshire, where the Rev. Hathersley was murdered.

It was 14.1 miles, as the railway travels.

———

IN 1835, PARLIAMENT APPROVED the construction of the Great Western Railway (GWR) between London and Bristol, 118 miles directly west of the capital. Six years later, the GWR authorized the building of a locomotive repair works on the line. A convenient location for the facility was identified as the junction of the western railway and the Golden Valley line.

That location was Swindon in Wilts, and the facility was named the Swindon Works. Once the Works was completed, Swindon began a transformation from a small market town to a "railway town." Swindon could also be connected with the Somerset Coalfield via a local canal—an efficient way to move coal for the steam locomotives. Thus, the town became an ideal site for operations of the western railway.

Scarlet checked the Great Western Railway schedules now, and realized Swindon had another attraction in terms of his investigation of the Hathersley murder. It was the perfect location for anyone wishing to get to Lambourn and back quickly and without any fuss.

"DO YOU KEEP RECORDS of the major magic shows that give performances in England?"

Scarlet was sitting in the neatly-kept office in the Robert-Houdin Club of the neatly bald Mr. Farley Dolman, the Club's Museum and Records Director, who sat at his desk with his hands folded neatly in front of him.

Mr. Dolman was neatly bald on top, with an unusually sharp divide between the end of his baldness and his fringe hair on either side, as though it was carefully kept that way with a razor. Perhaps it was.

"Of course, we do. We are a museum, after all, as well as a private club."

The director of records had a crisp and clipped speech pattern, as though words were expensive and he was careful in doling them out.

"Would you mind explaining to me what those records include?"

"Perhaps you might explain to *me* the nature of your inquiry."

"Perhaps you'd be more comfortable continuing this conversation at Scotland Yard headquarters."

Scarlet rarely played the 'or-would-you-like-to-go-down-to-the-station' card. But something about this fellow grated on his nerves.

Dolman gave it a pause, but he clipped that off too.

"We keep records of the run of a show and any local personnel hired, along with businesses that are engaged for things like costumes and transportation. We clip notices from the newspapers, naturally, along with any charitable appearances by the performers. We also pay special attention to any unique tricks or illusions associated with that magician."

That was what Scarlet was hoping to hear.

"I see. Are you familiar with the "Your Fondest Wish" segment of Max von Leiden's show?"

"Certainly."

"And is that illusion one of the things you'd have a record of? I mean concerning the current run of *Phantasmagoria*?"

Mr. Dolman leaned forward over his hands, which were still clasped on the desktop. "With all due respect, Dr. Scarlet," he said with a half-smile that nevertheless looked painful, "if you tell me exactly what you're looking for, I will be glad to help you if I can."

"I'm interested in the names of the audience volunteers who participated in the 'Your Fondest Wish' segment during this tour of the show. Is that something the Club's museum keeps a record of?"

"Perhaps," said Dolman, somewhat carefully, thought Scarlet. "And it's the current U.K. tour we're talking about, not Herr von Leiden's other seasons performing this segment of his show?"

"Yes, that's right."

"You realize that anyone's name we might have will only be in connection with their appearance as a volunteer in the show. We have no information about their private lives."

Once more, Scarlet told Dolman that he was correct.

"Well, then you're in luck. 'Your Fondest Wish' is, of course, a signature illusion of Max von Leiden's show. As such, we consider it an essential part of the historical record. I'll be happy to retrieve that information for you. Please wait here."

Dolman stood, and now that he had prolonged the granting of his permission as long as possible, he exited the room quickly.

The annoying little Cock of the Walk.

———————

HE RETURNED FIFTEEN MINUTES later brandishing a single sheet of paper. He handed it to the still-seated Scarlet, and instead of going back behind his desk, stood beside the chair as his guest looked it over.

Scarlet paid no attention to him.

He'd seen what he was looking for immediately.

Two minutes later, he stood at the top of the steps outside the Robert-Houdin Club, the now-folded sheet of paper in his inside pocket. He was looking at St Martin's Lane but not really seeing it.

Three lines of inquiry were converging in his mind's eye.

They were like three separate train lines, all leading to the same station.

CHAPTER 22

The Wish List

carlet swayed with the rhythm of the hansom cab taking him to the Queen Victoria Theatre Royal. The lines from a poem in an old play kept running in his head:

Golden lads and girls all must,
As chimney-sweepers, come to dust.

He was thinking—he could not stop thinking—about the list of names he was now carrying in his inside coat pocket.

One thing about the Methuselah Plague victims had bothered him from the start. As far as the investigators had been able to determine, the people who had succumbed to the disease had had nothing in common,. Geographically, or in terms of genetics, sex, lifestyle, diet, etc., there wasn't anything that researchers could hang their hat on. There was certainly nothing like a shared habit, which is how John Snow discovered in 1854 that users of a single water pump on Broad Street were falling victim to the cholera bacteria present in that water.

Yet a widely divergent population in different countries had all aged rapidly and died quickly—all of them coming to dust, just like in the lines of the poem.

He had felt that the more he thought like an epidemiologist

rather than a biologist, the closer he seemed to be getting to the truth. But it hadn't come. Still, the idea that it was the *population* involved, rather than their habits, had tantalized and frustrated him in equal measure.

"In the fields of observation chance favors only the prepared mind," the French chemist Louis Pasteur had declared in 1854—coincidentally the same year as Dr. Snow's epidemiological breakthrough. Scarlet's mind had been prepared in precisely that way, though he hadn't been aware of it.

But two things which happened within minutes of each other had landed softly but richly on the field of this thinking, which was already 'prepared.' Django's note had reminded him of the final gala performance of 'Your Fondest Wish' before Leiden's show left town. And Bilby's report had arrived, detailing *Phantasmagoria*'s tour at the end of last year before it arrived in London.

Where people began dying of the Methuselah Plague.

Bilby *always* exceeded his brief in terms of "data" supplied—it was a source of pride for him—and his report had contained more information on von Leiden's tour than Scarlet had asked for. He had glanced at those pages but hadn't thought them important for his purposes. He did now. The pages included dates and locations for *Phantasmagoria*'s international bookings.

Before its current English tour, the show had appeared in France, Germany, and the United States. As it happened, these were the same three countries where the Plague had shown up outside of the United Kingdom.

THE BACKSTAGE AREA OF the Queen Victoria theatre was the scene of the same controlled chaos that it had been on Scarlet's previous visit, ten days earlier. This time, however, he and Max von Leiden didn't shake hands when he entered the latter's dressing room.

The magician didn't seem particularly surprised to see him. For one thing, the temperature of his personality hadn't risen by a single degree. He showed his current contempt by keeping his seat while making Scarlet stand. The latter didn't care. It gave him the opportunity to look down on this self-proclaimed genius.

Despite the setting, Scarlet felt that he was in his element. If this were a script, he thought, his first line was a good one, and he delivered it with relish.

"I would be interested if you told me how you killed Giuseppe Caliosto."

Herr Von Leiden, applying his makeup, laughed.

"I'm sorry, Dr. Scarlet. But really. If you had any evidence to back such a scurrilous claim, you wouldn't ask me such a question. You would simply arrest me."

"There's still time."

"Ah, well. Nothing is more terrible than ignorance in action—to quote Goethe. I have all the time in the world, sir. Do you?"

Let the great man play his games of insults and arrogance. Let him be at his ease and confident. Scarlet had begun the questioning with the Caliosto murder because it was, in fact, the weakest card in his desk. He had no evidence to make the claim that von Leiden was involved in Marco the Magnificent's death. But that wasn't why he was here.

Detectives and police officers had a game of their own. If they had enough to arrest a suspect, they did, and it was the Crown's business to deal with the criminal after that. But when they had no proof but believed in their gut that a suspect was guilty, that's when they began to push. There were many ways to apply pressure until cracks appeared in a suspect's façade of innocence. Once that happened, the suspect's behavior could change in any number of ways. You just had to try to be prepared for as many of them as you could.

Scarlet had a moment of *déjà vu*. Here they were, exactly as they had been in their previous conversation, having a discussion in von Leiden's dressing room as the master applied his makeup. But things would not turn out like the last time.

Von Leiden had said that he had all the time in the world.

"It's interesting that you should say that, sir," Scarlet said now. "I've seen your act, and time plays tricks in one of them, doesn't it?"

"My dear Doctor. If you knew anything about magic, you would know that all tricks depend upon timing."

"I didn't say timing. I said time."

"Ah, good. It's a much more interesting subject, isn't it?"

"Yes, it is. Tell me, how is it that you can manipulate it?"

"I haven't the slightest idea what you're referring to."

"'Your Fondest Wish,' Herr von Leiden. Your most famous trick."

"I have been known for many famous illusions in my career."

"But nothing quite like that one—isn't that right? The way the person you've mesmerized tells their story, and immediately people from their past appear behind the scrim acting out those scenes. I told my companion the evening that I saw your show that from a theatrical standpoint that was impossible."

"That's magic, my friend."

"No it isn't, my *friend*. You're somehow manipulating time."

Von Leiden stopped patting his cheek with powder and looked at Scarlet in the mirror. "You're a man of science. Tell me: how could I do such a thing?"

"Perhaps we'll find out in your grand finale on the 6th of July—your final performance in London. You plan a 'procession' featuring all of this season's 'Your Fondest Wish' participants, don't you?"

A slight smile—ghoulish because of the white cake makeup on the face.

"That's right. You will be in the audience, I hope. If you don't have tickets—"But Scarlet had handed von Leiden a sheet of paper from his pocket.

"Do you recognize these names?"

The magician glanced at the list and handed it back to Scarlet. "Yes, of course. Those are all the audience volunteers that have appeared in the illusion this season."

"And you claim that all of them will be part of the grand procession in your final performance?"

"The English volunteers. Yes, I do claim that. Why is that a problem, Doctor?"

"It's a problem, sir, because all of these people are dead. This is a list of the victims of The Methuselah Plague in the United Kingdom. And every one of them was a participant in your 'Fondest Wish' illusion."

Scarlet let that statement sink in.

"Would you tell me, Herr von Leiden, how you plan to bring people back from the grave to perform in your show?"

———

SCARLET WASN'T SURE WHAT he expected. A sudden furious rage, perhaps, with a sweep of an arm sending all the makeup pots and jars crashing to the floor. Or better yet, a startling magical illusion! Herr von Leiden suddenly towering over Scarlet and reaching down for him with a giant hand. Or much better still—a dragon soaring into the room and carrying von Leiden away on its back, with the great magician never to be seen or heard from again.

But not this casual response to his devastating question.

This grave, immense, blasé answer.

"You and everyone else will understand then, Dr. Scarlet."

"Understand what, sir?"

"What a truly great magician is capable of."

CHAPTER 23

A Strong Accusation

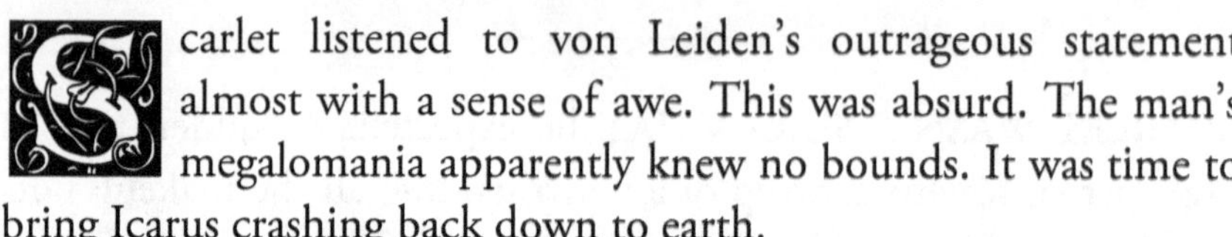carlet listened to von Leiden's outrageous statement almost with a sense of awe. This was absurd. The man's megalomania apparently knew no bounds. It was time to bring Icarus crashing back down to earth.

"Be that as it may, I'm here for another reason as well. I wonder if you'll tell me what your relationship was with Mr. John Roach?"

"Charming name," said the magician as he began to work on his left eye with an eyeliner pencil. Would the man never finish with his infernal makeup? "I gather from your clever questioning method that I am supposed to know this fellow."

"Do you?"

"Not that I'm aware of. Unless, of course, I've stepped on him without realizing it. Is that what you're going to arrest me for?"

"I have here an itinerary of your English tour, at the end of last year and the beginning of this year."

Von Leiden was leaning close to the mirror to examine his left eye closely. Evidently it passed muster, as he started applying the eyeliner to his right eyelid.

"You surprise me, Doctor. I didn't know you went in for magic. How many other documents are you going to produce from that ordinary-looking frock coat?"

"You played Swindon from December 8th to the 15th. That's in Wiltshire. Do you remember that booking?"

"Vaguely. Why?"

"Did you stay in Swindon the entire time you were there?"

"I suppose so. Frankly, I don't recall the town at all. And I certainly don't remember how I spent every one of my free hours six months ago in the provinces. Aside from the performances, that is. Which if you must know, is basically all I recall about any place where we do the show."

"You didn't take a quick train ride to Lambourn, perhaps?"

"Where is Lambourn? And why would I take a 'quick train ride' there?"

"It's a village in the county of Berkshire. It's fourteen miles from Swindon."

"*That* I am delighted to learn. And why would I have taken this enchanting train ride to a place I've never heard of before?"

"To commit a murder."

Now, the Master of Illusion—in full makeup at last—stood and faced his visitor.

"This is the third time you've crossed my path, Dr. William Scarlet. I vowed at the Club that there would not be a third time. I am remiss. But now you've gone from insinuating questions to making slanderous charges. Unfortunately, there are no witnesses to it. No matter. It is a dangerous business to take me on as an opponent. Mind that fact, sir."

"Yes, I've seen your physical strength, Herr von Leiden."

"What do you mean by that?"

"I mean, you have the strength to kill a man with your hands."

"What man? Who are you talking about?"

"John Roach. You didn't step on him. You used your hands to crush his skull."

"Why would I do such a thing?"

"Because he was blackmailing you."

"Really? For what?"

"For the murder of the Rev. Charles Hathersley at St Michael and All the Angels church in Lambourn, Berkshire. Where you arrived on the train from Swindon and got back again before that day's evening performance."

"I hope you have evidence to back up such a claim, Dr. Scarlet—and that it was in your superiors' hands before you came here to make that charge."

"Oh, I do, Herr von Leiden. And it has been, since earlier today."

———

STEPPING OUT OF THE building into bustling Haymarket Street, and then the wide thoroughfare of Pall Mall, seemed to Scarlet like coming back to life after a too-close encounter with evil.

But he'd accomplished what he came here to do.

This too was part of the detective game.

Someone you knew was guilty was now on notice.

An investigation into a magic trick that somehow aged people prematurely and then killed them—with no evidence yet to support such a claim—was the kind of inquiry perhaps only Scarlet's own Society for Supernatural and Psychic Research could carry on.

Intentional homicide performed on a victim with observable injuries, however, was something else entirely.

The evidence from the *Phantasmagoria* itinerary; the timing of Roach's departure from Lambourn and his arrival in London where the magic show would shortly be appearing; and the manner of Roach's death—all were being looked into by the Yard.

Von Leiden was aware of that now.

Let the cracks begin to appear in that façade of innocence.

CHAPTER 24

The Thing From Two Points of View

 have a job for you," Scarlet told Django Pierce-Jones two days later. It had taken him that amount of time to come up with the plan.

"Hold your houses, old fellow," said Django.

This was another unfortunate instance of his half-Romani friend employing a typical British expression and not getting away with it.

"That's 'horses,'" Scarlet corrected him: "Hold your *horses*. How could you possibly hold a house?"

"Oh, yes! I see what you mean. Whatever you say, dear boy. But explain all of this to me again. You suspect Herr von Leiden of how many murders? And you have proof of some but not others?"

The two of them were walking in Whitehall Gardens near Scarlet's office. It was difficult to believe that the park had been laid out just fourteen years ago, in 1875. At the moment, they were on the path between the statues of General Sir James Outram and Sir Henry Bartle Frere. The springtime masses of tulips were gone from the plot in front of the Frere statue, and now in late June there was nothing in their place. "Why the devil don't they plant roses?" thought Scarlet, then realized he sounded just like Django in one of his fervently British moments.

"That's right," he replied. "I'm afraid we may never have any proof that von Leiden had a hand in Marco the Magnificent's death during The Bullet Catch. A magician would probably know more than one way to sabotage a dangerous trick his rival was performing, especially a past-master like von Leiden."

"And the girl—Frances Murch?"

"Unfortunately, making someone unhappy enough to kill themselves isn't prosecutable. Or perhaps it is. But we have absolutely no evidence."

"So what evidence do you have that your so-lenient English courts would allow you to introduce?"

"Careful," Scarlet warned, "or you'll be asked to stand for a seat from the Liberal Unionist Party . . . if not as an outright Conservative!"

The two friends laughed.

"It's the Roach murder that points more directly to Herr von Leiden," Scarlet explained to Django. "We have the location of the *Phantasmagoria* tour in Swindon on the day of the Rev. Hathersley's death in Lambourn, fourteen miles away. The priest was murdered in the early hours of the morning of December 14th last. There was a morning train leaving Lambourn that day that would have brought von Leiden back to Swindon in plenty of time for the show's Friday evening performance."

"Is that enough to bring a case?"

"No, it isn't," Scarlet admitted. It's all circumstantial. With circumstantial evidence, you can only prove indirectly that someone committed a crime. And even then, you need more of it than we have."

Django nodded. A moment later, he asked:

"How did you get on to Herr von Leiden concerning the priest's death in the first place?"

"John Roach's murder, a week ago. Roach was an assistant custodian at the St Michael and All the Angels Church, which is what led me to Lambourn. But he left the church's employ—left town, in fact—immediately after Rev. Hathersley's murder.

"There are two reasons Roach would do that, as far as I can see: either he killed the vicar himself, or he knew who did and figured he had to get away. Of the two alternatives, I think it's much more likely that von Leiden seized the opportunity to come down by train from the nearby town where he was performing and commit the murder."

"But why?"

"I don't know the answer to that yet. But I can surmise that there was some kind of enmity between von Leiden and Rev. Hathersley. Herr von Leiden has shown his cruelty many times before now, on stage and off—Bilby's dossier has plenty of evidence of it. And he openly blasphemes on stage. It wouldn't surprise me in the least to find out that there was a mutual hatred between the dark magician and an Anglican cleric—and that von Leiden took the opportunity his schedule provided to do something about it."

"And his reason for killing Roach?"

"Blackmail. Roach relocated to London right after the murder. This is where the magic show would be arriving six weeks later—the tour schedule was printed on all the posters. If he witnessed Rev. Hathersley's murder, this would be the perfect place for him to hide. He could get lost far more easily in the city than in the village of Lambourn.

"We know he stayed in doss houses for the first six weeks, so he must have been as poor as a church mouse . . . sorry, I'm not trying to be witty. But all he would have to do is wait for *Phantasmagoria* to arrive. A famous magician like Max von Leiden would surely pay up to prevent Roach from going to the police about the Hathersley murder. And as far as I've been able to find out, Roach's doss house days ended at the same time *Phantasmagoria* came to town. His prospects appear to have improved considerably starting at the end of January. So the timing works out perfectly."

"But the tour arrived in London six months ago. Why kill Roach now?"

"Convenience? Or perhaps the right opportunity came along."

"But why leave the body of the blackmailer you've just killed behind The Robert-Houdin Club? Isn't that . . . what do you say, a giveaway?"

"Yes: *dead giveaway* is what we say. But that's von Leiden's arrogance, you see. And there's another reason that explains why Roach was killed now. I first interviewed Herr von Leiden twelve days ago, on June 14th. Roach was found in the alley a few minutes after midnight on June 18th. Our German friend may have decided he didn't like our conversation of a few days earlier, and thought it was time to teach me a lesson."

They had found a seat on a wooden bench. As he sat, Django Pierce-Jones thought about what Scarlet had said while looking down at the path at his feet. When he looked up, his expression had changed.

"What about the other matter you mentioned to me? The biggest mystery, I would say. You said you thought Max von Leiden is responsible for the deaths of all the people from the Methuselah Plague. How is that possible?"

"I don't know that yet," his friend admitted. "But let's focus first on the murder we may be able to prove."

"But surely this is of much greater import."

"One impossible solution at a time, my friend," advised Scarlet.

"I said I had a job for you," he continued a moment later. "Are you interested?"

"Famously," replied Django. Whatever the slight disconnect between the question and the answer, Scarlet understood.

"Good. I want you to talk to the stage manager at the Queen Victoria Theatre Royal. He's a chap by the name of Daley Swanson. Everyone calls him Dabbs. I've never met him, but J.N. Maskelyne gave me his name. I want you to feel him out concerning what goes on backstage during the 'Your Fondest Wish' segment of *Phantasmagoria*."

"You don't want to ask him yourself?"

Scarlet shook his head.

"I can't take the chance that von Leiden would see me. Or someone else in the show that might mention me to him, for that matter. I've been backstage twice now. I'm guessing my face is well known by now as someone the star of the show is at odds with."

"But why would a member of the crew of this show reveal anything to me about Herr von Leiden's secrets?"

"He's not a member of the crew. He's the permanent stage manager for the theatre, not the show. Any act on tour that is booked into a theatre has to hire local talent for the backstage work, transporting the equipment, and other tasks. It would be far too expensive to keep people like that in their employ. Dabbs Swanson will have no loyalty to the *Phantasmagoria* show."

"But he might like von Leiden and refuse to talk to me."

"He doesn't like him, according to Maskelyne. Evidently, von Leiden treats everyone the way he treated Frances Murch. This will help make Swanson willing to talk to you."

Scarlet handed Pierce-Jones a £1 banknote.

"I want you to find out everything you can about how 'Your Fondest Wish' works from a backstage perspective. Von Leiden will have had to show the Theatre Royal's stage manager and crew the secrets of the illusion in terms of mechanics and any machinery and lighting effects used. Will you do it?"

"With pleasure."

Scarlet patted Django's knee.

"That's my boy. If you can manage to meet Mr. Swanson outside of the theatre, so much the better. If not, let's think of a plausible reason for you to be poking your nose around backstage."

"Why poking my nose? That's something that would be noticed. I'll make a legitimate appointment with Mr. Swanson. I'll say I write for the monthly magazine *The Theatre*. We're planning an issue on the great magic shows that transcend the music halls and get booked into the major theatres. I'll say that interest has been heightened since the tragedy of Marco the Magnificent's death during his signature illusion."

"Yes, that's excellent. Do you think you can get away with it?"

"You don't think I'm suave enough to pull it off?"

Scarlet, laughing, realized that Django had him there.

SCARLET DIDN'T EXPECT THAT his second meeting of the day, with his superior, Dr. Mallinson, would be as pleasant or as successful. As it happened, he was right on both counts.

Sir Edward Mallinson, M.D., was the kind of man you often found in leadership positions in Victoria's government, exuding the authority of the British Empire. Scarlet had often wondered how many of Her Majesty's appointments were due to the similarity of a gentleman's physical appearance to that of the Queen's beloved late husband, Prince Albert of Saxe-Coburg and Gotha, who had died of typhoid fever back in 1861 at the still-vigorous age of 42.

Mallinson was the very model of these bureaucrats stamped in the Prince Albert mold: tall with a long pointed nose and even longer side whiskers, a small mustache, and unwavering blue eyes. Unlike Victoria's late husband, however, Mallinson still had hair. Lots of it, in fact, wavy and steel grey. Mallinson was one of those chaps who looked like he might have led the Charge of the Light Brigade, had that event not been thirty-five years earlier, and had he chosen a generalship instead of a career in medicine.

It didn't take long for Scarlet to know which way the wind was blowing on the heights of Olympus today.

"What makes you think this lot is enough to refer this case to the Crown?" said Mallinson, leaning back in his desk chair and indicating the papers before him with the eyeglasses he was holding in his right hand.

It was always like this with Mallinson, whom Scarlet knew perfectly well had a strong bias against him. As Chief Surgeon of the Metropolitan Police, Mallinson was aware of—and thoroughly despised—his subordinate's power of *psychometry*. Scarlet's ability to experience visions and the inner life of another person from touching them or an object they'd handled was anathema to Mallinson. As far as he was concerned, occult powers had no place in a police investigation.

The irony was that Scarlet was scrupulous about keeping his psychometry separate from his regular duties, and tried never to use it in an official investigation. But either Mallinson couldn't see that, or suspected that his assistant surgeon was using his power behind his back. Scarlet didn't give a damn about his boss's attitude as far as his personal life and abilities were concerned. But he knew he had to keep his face clean concerning any evidence he uncovered, not only with Mallinson but with the Crown Prosecutor's office.

At any rate, that hadn't happened in the John Roach murder case. But it didn't matter much one way or the other if the evidence was thin.

Which was exactly what his boss was reminding him of now.

"Do you seriously expect us to go forward with *this*?"

"I know it's circumstantial, sir."

"It's a damn sight worse than that. In our justice system, Dr. Scarlet, circumstantial evidence is best used to fill in the gaps in a prosecution's case. It shouldn't be the whole case."

"But when you put it all together—"

"Put what together? As far as I can see, you have a suspect that can be proven to have been fourteen miles from the scene of a murder. All right, he happens to be a very strong man, perhaps strong enough to crush a man's skull. But there's no proof that that's what happened.

"Then you have someone who left a town in Berkshire where another murder occurred and moved to London before a magic show arrived so that he could blackmail the show's famous magician. What blackmail? Where's the evidence for that? Christ, talk about weak tea!" He tossed his glasses down on top of the report on the desk and shook his head. "If you can't come up with solid evidence without practicing your bloody witchcraft, I'll have to reassign you to clinical duties only."

This was grossly unfair, and Scarlet could feel the tips of his ears burning.

He could admit to himself that he had stronger reasons for pursuing Max von Leiden—not only for this murder but the others—than the Roach evidence showed. But how could he explain to Mallinson what he'd felt and seen when he shook the magician's hand? He hadn't been thinking of using his power at that moment . . . and he certainly couldn't share his sensation with the mocking Mallinson now. He'd seen what he called an *absolute darkness*—unlike any other psychometric sensation he'd ever experienced before. There was no vision, no thoughts, no emotions: only complete silence and *nothingness*.

The experience had frightened him then. But now he thought that it was freeing him.

Yes, it was always this way with Mallinson. The cases that Scarlet and Pierce-Jones found themselves investigating were always ones that the Metropolitan Police would decline to pursue, if they had known about them. The fact was, the Yard *couldn't* pursue them—for it wasn't equipped to do so; and it would only have been confused and disoriented if it had tried.

Scarlet and Pierce-Jones's gentlemen's club, The Society for Supernatural and Psychic Research, and the other hand, had been founded specifically to investigate cases of the unknown and supernatural that the authorities couldn't. And there was a reason it had chosen the psychic Scarlet and the medium Pierce-Jones as its field investigators.

The Society's unique mission was once again in play on this case. It would have to take the lead in discovering what Max von Leiden was really up to.

That was the simple truth of the matter.

CHAPTER 25

A Visitor from the Darkness

n the twenty-seventh of June—two days after his meetings with Pierce-Jones and Dr. Mallinson—Scarlet received a telegram at his office. It was from Nine Columns, the Wilsons' home on Beatrice Road in Finsbury Park.

The handwritten message on the Post Office Telegraphs form was brief. It read:

Disquieting incident here. Can you come immediately?
Margaret Wilson

Margaret Wilson was Catherine and Elizabeth's mother and the wife of Hiram Wilson, head of the country's Railway Department. The telegram was disturbing and confusing for Scarlet. Why in the world would Mrs. Wilson be contacting him? He could imagine Catherine sending him a note—perhaps even an urgent telegram— but not her mother.

This time he didn't walk out to Whitehall and hail a cab. Instead, he took one of the hansoms-with-driver that the Yard kept on hand for last-minute transportation around London, and was at Nine Columns thirty minutes later.

———————

SCARLET HANDED HIS HAT to the maid and entered the Wilsons' drawing room, with its mint-green walls and blue chairs and rug that he knew so well. Catherine was seated on the sofa with the flower print across from the windows. She looked up as he entered, her anxious expression dissolving when she saw him.

But her face was deathly pale. Scarlet resisted the urge to go to her at once to take her pulse and feel if her skin was cold and sweaty, for he didn't warn to alarm the family. Yet Catherine looked like she might faint at any moment. Her sister Elizabeth sat at her side, holding her hand, and beside Lizzie stood her husband, Ambrose. Mrs. Wilson occupied the settee that was the twin of the sofa, placed diagonally in front of one of the windows across the room.[*]

"Oh, Dr. Scarlet!" said Margaret Wilson, who had been the first to see him from her position directly opposite the door. She crossed to him and took his hand in both of hers. "Thank you. We're so grateful you could come."

"William," said Catherine, more softly. Scarlet immediately took the few steps to the sofa and sat down beside her.

"What's all this, then? What's going on?" he said. "You look like you've seen a ghost."

"No, not that," Catherine replied. "I wish I had."

Elizabeth spoke up: "We had a visitor who frightened Lizzie half to death."

"Here? This afternoon?"

Catherine took up the narrative herself.

"Yes, a little over an hour ago. Mother and Elizabeth were . . . somewhere else in the house, I don't remember now. Anyway, the maid handed me a calling card which had the Railway Department's design printed on it, and the name Aldred Leeper.

---

[*] See *Red Season* (Cedar & Maitland Press, 2024), Book #1 in the Dr. William Scarlet Mysteries, for the first appearance of Ambrose Reed and the Wilsons: Elizabeth, Catherine, Margaret, and Hiram.

"I came into this room to greet him, thinking that whoever it was must want Father. But he was at work, of course. I thought it was silly of someone to come calling here, when he would have been much better off asking someone at the Railway Department where Father could be found. And this Mr. Leeper was sitting where Mother is now, and stood up when I came into the room."

Now Catherine's brow furrowed and her mouth took on a distasteful shape.

"He was hideous. His face . . ." and she hesitated.

"Was it disfigured?" asked Scarlet, thinking like a doctor.

"No. But it wasn't normal. He had these awful black eyes. This sounds mad, but I'd swear that his eyes didn't have any irises, just pupils. Huge black pupils. It was quite disorienting." She looked at him. "Have you ever seen a patient with eyes like that, William?"

"There is a condition—"

"It was evil, somehow. These eyes with enormous pupils like shiny black marbles, looking at you and through you. You can generally tell what a person is thinking or feeling from the look in their eyes, but I couldn't see anything there—just these two enormous black marbles looking at me."

"Did he approach you—did he touch you?"

"No, thank God. He'd stood when I entered, but he sat back down when we started talking."

"What did he look like otherwise? Age, height, weight, complexion?"

"He looked *stunted*. I know that doesn't make any sense, but that's the impression I got when he stood up as I came into the room." She closed her eyes, re-imagining the man she'd seen. "He had an unusually wide face, and a pig-like nose. His complexion was red and mottled, and he had dark red hair, very thick." She opened her eyes. "I'm sure I couldn't tell you how old he was within even a decade. He was simply frightening to look at."

"What did he say?"

"Just that he was here to see Father and was sorry he had missed him, and would I mention that he was here? And he pointed to his calling card that I was still holding in my hand."

She looked at the others. "Doesn't it all seem odd?"

"In what way, dear?" asked Mrs. Wilson.

"It's like he wanted me to see him—that he came here deliberately to frighten me. What do you think, William?"

"That's exactly what I think," he told her.

"Why would anyone do that?"

Scarlet thought he knew the answer to that question too, though he didn't tell Catherine now. He took her right hand in his to comfort her.

The vision hit him immediately. He was glad that, after all these years of his *psychometry* kicking in when he could not expect it, he could control his flinching at the mental and physical shock that came with suddenly experiencing another's life.

He saw Catherine, decades older than she was now. She looked to be near death. Her face was only a hollow shell, and her soft skin was wasted away. Her beauty had been ravaged.

That was as much as he wanted to see of this vision. As gently as he could, he let go of her hand. Then he looked at her, wearing what he hoped was a reassuring smile.

He was certain now of why the rather monstrous Mr. Leeper had paid a visit to the Wilsons.

CHAPTER 26

A Refuge In a Time of Danger

ill you do it?" asked Scarlet.

He was standing in Pierce-Jones's front parlour, looking down at Django who sat at the mahogany and marble table in the center of the room. The morning coffee service was still set on the table, though the breakfast dishes had been cleared away.

"Of course I will. I'll protect her with my life. Now settle yourself, old chum, and sit back down."

But Scarlet continued to pace with his arms crossed. "'Old chum' yourself," he said. "Anyway, I certainly hope you won't have to. I'm going to speak to Sgt. Jessey and ask him to keep an eye on this place."

"Good choice. Are you expecting trouble from Herr von Leiden or this fellow Leeper?"

Now Scarlet did sit back down. He sipped his coffee, which was cold.

"Either. Both. I don't really know. But I'm convinced that our German friend has Catherine in his line of sight now—and that that's a very dangerous place to be."

Pierce-Jones's interview with Dabbs Swanson, the stage manager at the Queen Victoria, hadn't turned up anything useful. There was a simple yet frustrating reason for that: the 'Your Fondest

Wish' illusion didn't depend on any machinery or device, as most magicians' major tricks do. So there were no secrets to the illusion that the stage manager had been able to share. At any rate, it seemed unimportant now, given what had occurred at the Wilsons' residence yesterday.

"I understand," said Django. "What should I be on the lookout for?"

"I don't know that either. Keep your revolver close at hand."

"Ah, well. — Do y'think it will do any good against a fiend?"

Scarlet was sure that Pierce-Jones meant it as a joke and didn't answer. He didn't think it was funny, though, and for a very disturbing feeling that was growing inside him.

No, not funny at all.

"Anything else?" asked Django.

"Just keep that revolver handy."

———————

SGT. JAMES JESSEY WAS a stalwart veteran of the Metropolitan Police of many years' standing. He was a gruff and no-nonsense character who gave the impression that he was carved out of solid bedrock, but whom Scarlet knew to really be a devoted family man. To those outside of the police and criminal worlds, Jessey seemed like the proverbial copper who did everything by the book. They had no way of knowing, of course, how often he bent it—sometimes so much so that it was hardly recognizable as a book anymore.

Scarlet and Jessey were strolling on the walkway adjoining the Horse Guards Parade outside Whitehall. The setting, as much as the conversation, was an indicator that Scarlet's request didn't originate inside official channels.

"You want me to keep an eye out then, sir," Jessey said as they walked. "Should I pull one or two lads out of regular duty as well?"

"No, sergeant. I need this to stay as quiet as possible. More than one man would be too conspicuous. Do a walk-by whenever you can fit it into your schedule."

"Right, sir. Who or what am I looking out for?"

"I can answer the 'who' part of that question, but not the 'what.' There are two scoundrels you need to stay awake for. Do you know who Max von Leiden is?"

"The magician?"

"Yes, that's the man I mean. He's dangerous, sergeant. I have him in my sights for the case of the man who was found with his skull crushed."

Scarlet knew that Jessey wasn't easily impressed; but he seemed so now.

"Is he up for it, sir? Then how can he be out?"

"No, he isn't in custody. And we won't get him there without more evidence than we have now. But he knows I'm onto him. The net is getting smaller, and I'm not at all sure how he'll react. He may show up at Mr. Pierce-Jones's house, which is why I want you to be on the sly."

"Why would that be, sir?"

"Why would he show up at the house?"

Jessey nodded.

"That's where someone I believe is one of his henchmen comes in, a man named Aldred Leeper."

"Odd name, sir, isn't it?"

"It is. But the man himself is stranger still, I'm told. He's rather hideous looking, so you shouldn't have any trouble recognizing him. He looks 'stunted,' as the person who saw him describes him. He has dark red hair, a wide face with a pig-like nose, and odd eyes that look like black marbles."

"Crickey!" said Sgt. Jessey. "What's a bloke like that doing on the streets? Did he escape from an asylum?"

"It rather sounds that way, doesn't it? Leeper showed up at the Wilsons' home yesterday and scared Catherine Wilson half to death. I'm convinced he's in the employ of Herr von Leiden—and that he succeeded in his mission of warning me by intimidating someone I know. I've arranged for Miss Wilson to stay with Mr. Pierce-Jones for the moment."

"I see, sir."

Scarlet smiled, and offered Sgt. Jessey his hand.

"Anything else you'd like to know, sergeant?"

"No, sir. Thank you, sir."

Scarlet walked back to his office, thinking that might be able to use the hand again normally in an hour or two.

CHAPTER 27

Hey, Presto!

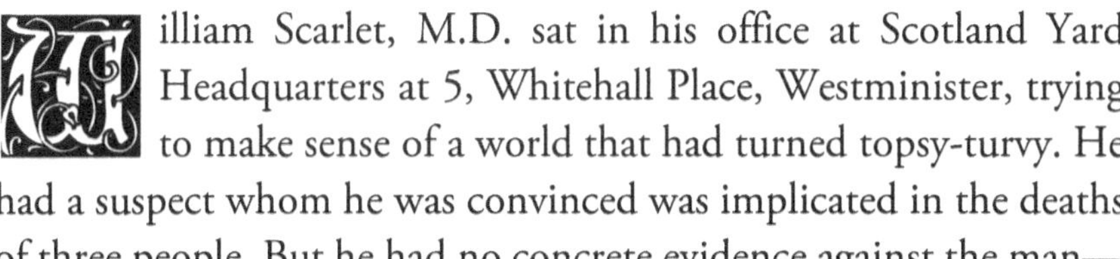illiam Scarlet, M.D. sat in his office at Scotland Yard Headquarters at 5, Whitehall Place, Westminister, trying to make sense of a world that had turned topsy-turvy. He had a suspect whom he was convinced was implicated in the deaths of three people. But he had no concrete evidence against the man—only a gut feeling backed by instinct.

No, it was stronger than that. He had a *moral certainty* that Max von Leiden was dangerously psychopathic. The term had been current for the last forty years or so, and it seemed the perfect word to describe the German magician. But his feeling about von Leiden surpassed even that. He rarely used the word *evil* with regard to a suspect, or even thought it. Yet this man was evil.

On top of this unusually strong moral response of his, there was a monstrous certainty in his mind that he couldn't deny, no matter that it too seemed unreasonable. He believed that this magician— or whatever he was—had carried out a murderous campaign, masked as an 'illusion,' that had killed great numbers of people.

His certainty came with the knowledge that the roll of 'Your Fondest Wish' volunteers exactly matched the list of victims of the Methuselah Plague. How this was possible, or why von Leiden had committed mass murder were questions he could not answer yet.

Just as bad, he knew these things to be true but couldn't do anything about them.

Was there a way he could force the magician's hand? And could he do it before next Saturday night, July 6th—exactly five days from now—after which *Phantasmagoria* would end its 1888-1889 season and von Leiden would be gone for good?

The thought of the show's finale reminded him of the other inconceivable possibility concerning Max von Leiden—that he would bring back all of the London season's participants in the 'Your Fondest Wish' illusion. He had strongly implied exactly that in their last meeting of a week ago.

But Scarlet knew that every one of those people was dead. The Master of Illusion would have to be an illusionist beyond mortal abilities to pull that trick off, and of course that was impossible.

What was his end-game, then, and what exactly was he trying to pull off?

Indeed, the world had turned upside down.

––––––––

AT LEAST THE WEEKEND had been quiet.

Pierce-Jones had informed him of that in a note he'd sent to Scarlet's house yesterday evening (Sunday). There had been no sign of von Leiden, the disturbing Aldred Leeper, or anyone else who might be deemed suspicious near Django's house.

The sergeant, in a telegram he'd sent, told Scarlet that he had checked in a few times over the weekend, but that he had nothing unusual to report. He informed Scarlet that Miss Wilson had asked after him, and seemed to be in good spirits.

Scarlet himself planned to get over there this afternoon, if he could spare the time. There were only five days now before von Leiden would presumably disappear, and the Yard still had no case against him that could be brought to court. The detective part of Scarlet wanted to slap bracelets on the man and have him securely in custody before then, and let the actual charge and the *Phantasmagoria* final gala performance both be damned. He couldn't deny, however, that the other part of him—the psychic part—was intrigued at how the great magician planned to carry off the impossible feat of bringing the dead back to life on stage.

Of course that could never happen. Von Leiden must be planning to simply give the illusion of doing so. The master conjurer would probably 'speak' with the spirits of the Methuselah Plague victims by manifesting them on stage—the way he had conjured the Mesopotamian goddess Ninlil in the performance Scarlet and Pierce-Jones attended. Hadn't he claimed in that performance that he was 'raising the dead'?

The thought of all of this magical mumbo-jumbo brought Scarlet back to earth. He made a conscious effort to clear his head—reminding himself that his task was to find evidence to convict a killer, not ooh and ah over spectacular parlour tricks, however expertly they were carried out.

His best chance of doing so was still the John Roach murder. Would von Leiden's sheer audacity and recklessness bring him down? He was deliberately flirting with danger in leaving Roach's body behind the magic club, no doubt excited by the psychopath's delusion that he was smarter than the police and looking for ways to prove it.

Of course I did it, he was telling them: *This is me, taunting you. And you ignorant jack-puddings will never be able to prove it.*

Well, prove it they must.

He had decided to proceed in two directions simultaneously. First, the Yard would simply have to beat the bushes more concerning anyone Roach had associated with in the six months he lived in London. If he was the kind of fellow who opened up when in his cups, for instance, there might be a mate of his or a girl who knew he was blackmailing the magician. Or someone may have seen the two of them talking at some point—von Leiden was, after all, an unmistakable figure.

The other direction was more clinical. He would access Kit Dickinson's records from the Roach autopsy. The thought had occurred to him that it might be possible to tie the skull fractures and plate displacements to a measurement of von Leiden's hands. It was admittedly a long-shot, but he thought it was worth a try.

He was just about to find Dickinson to discuss what he was looking for, when the Patrol Supervisor, Inspector John Cornish, came into his office with a serious look on his face.

"Dr. Scarlet, good morning. Have you heard from Sgt. Jessey? I believe he was working with you on a surveillance."

"No, I haven't. Is there a concern?"

"He didn't sign on for his shift this morning, and no one I've talked to here has seen him. I sent a patrolman to his home, but his wife said he didn't come home last night."

"I see. And she didn't think she should let us know?"

"Evidently it's not unusual. I gather Jessey keeps his own schedule, and sometimes stays out at night 'to check up on things,' as his wife put it. But he usually leaves a note to that effect, or has one of his men stop by the house to tell her. She said she had been telling herself not to worry when that hadn't happened yet today."

"And we queered the pitch, didn't we?"

"Yes, I'm afraid we did. If you hear something, let me know, won't you? There's a good fellow."

Scarlet followed Inspector Cornish out of his office by less than a minute. He was on his way to Pierce-Jones's house in Upper Grosvenor Street, a cold feeling in his stomach.

———

HE WAS YANKING THE bellpull when Django came up the steps from the street behind him.

"Where the devil have you been?" he said to him immediately.

"Getting a paper," Django replied, showing him the evidence. "I haven't been gone five minutes. What's wrong?"

"Is Catherine upstairs?"

"As far as I know. What is it? You look scared to death."

"Sgt. Jessey didn't show up for his shift this morning. I don't know it if has anything to do with his watching your house. For God's sake, why are we standing here talking? Let's get upstairs. . . . Ah, Wilfred," Scarlet said as the door was opened from inside. "Where's Miss Wilson?"

"I believe she's in the second floor parlour, sir," replied Django's manservant.

Scarlet and Django were both tall enough to take the stairs three at a time, calling out Catherine's name as they ascended. But Catherine wasn't in the second floor parlour. A very short time later, they realized she wasn't in the house at all.

"I'm very sorry, I'm sure, sir. I don't know where she could have gone," said an apprehensive-looking Wilfred a moment later.

"I'm not blaming you," Django assured him. "But think, man. Didn't you hear anything? The front door closing . . . anything?"

"I'm afraid not, sir."

"There were no visitors?"

"I would have told you that, sir," replied Wilfred, taking as much of a liberty in defending himself as he could.

Django looked at Scarlet.

"Five minutes," he said. "I swear it."

"I believe you," Scarlet replied. "You stay here. She may just have stepped out. I'll be back at the Yard. Send a messenger or telegram immediately you know something."

The cold feeling in Scarlet's stomach had turned into a block of ice.

Surprisingly, news about Sgt. Jessey was already waiting for him when he arrived back at his office in Whitehall Place. It was in the form of a note from Inspector Cornish, and couldn't have been briefer if words cost money. It read:

Jessey found. Reply at your earliest or come upstairs.

Found alive or dead?, you blithering idiot, Scarlet thought, even more on edge now than when he'd confronted Django on his front steps.

He went upstairs.

"He's alive," said Inspector John Cornish from behind his desk, as if could read the mind of the man striding into his office. Then again, any member of the Metropolitan Police would know the thoughts of a colleague in a situation like this. "He was found in a field at a place called Barnes Elm in Reading."

"In a field? In Reading, Berkshire?" said Scarlet with amazement. "I don't understand. That must be forty miles from here."

"Fifty, actually."

"But that's impossible. He was watching a house in Mayfair last night. Late last night, if I know Jessey. What does he say happened?"

"He's not saying anything. He can't. Didn't know where he was when they found him . . . didn't know his own name at first. Now all that's come back. But he has no idea what he's doing in that place or how he got there. I gather he's still rather in shock."

"Where is he, then?"

"Royal Berkshire Hospital. But I wouldn't go there if I were you. I'm sure he's in good medical hands."

"I wasn't planning to. I'll talk to him and examine him as soon as he gets here. Or are they going to keep him in hospital there?"

"I don't think they are," replied the inspector. "He's certainly in the dark though, poor chap." He made what sounded like a short, rueful laugh. "That's funny."

"What is?"

"What I just said, that Jessey's in the dark. The road the field is on where he was found is called Dark Lane."

CHAPTER 28

A Terrible Power

The next two days were agonizing and endless for Scarlet. Apart from his conversation with and examination of Sgt. Jessey—who had arrived back in London on Tuesday, July 2nd—there was nothing for him to do, no action that he could take. Canvassing of Django's neighborhood in Mayfair had been carried out vigorously, and every lead had been chased down by both the uniformed force and detectives. And no ransom demand or other communication had been received.

Herr von Leiden had been questioned, after an invented tip that the missing woman had been seen at the evening performance of *Phantasmagoria* the night before she disappeared. That gave Scotland Yard the excuse to interview everyone at the Queen Victoria Theatre Royal, Max von Leiden included. Scarlet wasn't present, of course, but he was briefed immediately afterwards.

There were no results, however, either from these interviews or any of the other actions the police were taking. Catherine Wilson seemed to have vanished from the face of the earth.

That thought was disturbingly close to Scarlet's reaction to the mystery of Jessey's disappearance and reappearance, in a dazed state fifty miles from where he was supposed to be. Both Jessey and Miss Wilson appeared to have been interfered with by something powerful and terrible. It confused and agitated Scarlet, and the implications of what it could be and do, frightened him.

He realized that the only person he could confide in without sounding insane was Django Pierce-Jones.

The two were talking now in the smoking room on the second floor of Pierce-Jones's house in Grosvenor Square. The house somehow seemed empty, even though Catherine Wilson had been staying there for less than three days before she disappeared.

At the same time, being here was a welcome change for Scarlet. He had spent literally every waking and sleeping moment since Monday in his office or in other areas of the Yard's headquarters building. Then he began thinking that there might be a clue in the house since this was the last place Catherine had been before she disappeared.

"Why not just bring him in?" said the Roma King. Scarlet's moods had been alternating over the past two days between agitation and gloom. Right now he was quiet and contemplative, and Django had chosen a good time to ask his question.

It took Scarlet a moment to shake off whatever he had been thinking, however.

"Sorry. What?"

"I asked why don't you put the man into custody?"

"On what charge? We have nothing to hold him on—never mind to bring before the assizes. Besides, you have no idea of what a ripping kick-up that will produce in the papers with someone as famous as Max von Leiden. The press will have a field day making us look like fools."

"There's nothing at all to tie him to Catherine's disappearance?"

"Not that we've found so far. He'll be leaving London after the last performance on Saturday, three days from now. If we don't find her before then, I don't know how we ever will. He could go anywhere in the world he wants to. And we already know that he's a master at hiding what he doesn't want others to see."

After a moment's pause, he added:

"But it's not just that, Django. There's something disturbing about the man that I can't quite put my hands on."

"How do you mean?"

"Haven't you noticed it? You're the one with the sensitive antennae. Don't you feel *something*? When I shook hands with him, I had a reaction. But I didn't see any visions or feel anything from him, the way I always do when my psychometry kicks in. There was literally nothing there—only blackness. I believe that means something in itself."

"In what sense?"

"I don't know!" said Scarlet. "That's the damnable thing—I just don't know!"

"Well, I admit he's strange. And yes, of course, I've felt that."

"It's not only strangeness. He's . . . powerful."

Now Scarlet looked Pierce-Jones in the eye.

"Did it ever occur to you that this magic act isn't his real power at all? That it's only a screen he's hiding behind, so we can't see what he's really capable of or what he's doing?"

"My God, Will—"

Scarlet went on before Pierce-Jones could finish that thought.

"Look at the evidence. How does he achieve that business in 'Your Fondest Wish,' for instance, of people from the audience volunteer's life appearing *at the same time they're being mesmerized to reveal their memories of the past*? There's something else I haven't mentioned to you. You know the whole point of this segment of the show is that people are supposed to achieve their fondest wish?"

"Yes, of course."

"Do you remember Margaret Sparrow: the audience volunteer the night we watched the show?"

"Vividly."

"She said she had a son, Johnny, who was in the Grenadier Guards. And when von Leiden asked her what her fondest wish was, she answered: 'It is to have my son, my Johnny, come home to me.'"

"I recall."

"I read a story in *The Times* recently. The Guards were posted to Cape Colony in South Africa, in the aftermath of the Jameson Raid. Private Sparrow was killed in a skirmish with Boer forces. So Mrs. Sparrow's 'fondest wish' of her Johnny coming home to her was fulfilled, though it was in a box."

"My God," Django repeated.

"It's worse than that. There's that unholy connection I told you about, between volunteering to participate in 'Your Fondest Wish' and contracting the Methuselah Plague afterwards. Every one of those people—*and only them*—has come down with the disease. How do we explain that?

"Well, I admit—"

"And I don't care how strong you are . . . how is it possible to crush a man's skull with your bare hands?"

Django tried again to interject. But Scarlet went on, continuing the litany of strange occurrences linked to Max von Leiden:

"Why murder a priest by crucifying him on an upside-down cross? You said you were gone for only five minutes on Monday morning."

"Yes. But what does—?"

"How could anyone arrive at your house, abduct a woman as spirited as Catherine Wilson—with your manservant home at the time—and then transport a police sergeant to a spot fifty miles away . . . all in the space of *five minutes*?"

The silence that followed these questions, hammered out one after the other, was a long one.

Finally, Django asked:

"Do you know what you're implying?"

"I know. Which is why we have to be at the theatre on Saturday night. I think he's planning to make Catherine part of his grand finale performance."

Pierce-Jones sounded shocked as he objected. "But why in the world would he do that? He knows the entire Metropolitan Police force is looking for her."

"Arrogance," Scarlet replied. "The same reason he left Roach's body behind the magician's club. It's the key to his personality . . . that, and cruelty. I don't think he can resist doing it—it's an essential part of the *tour de force* he wants to show the world."

He took a deep breath.

"That's why I have to convince Mallinson—and maybe even the new Commissioner, Monro himself—that we have to be at the Queen Victoria in force on Saturday night."

CHAPTER 29

Grand Finale

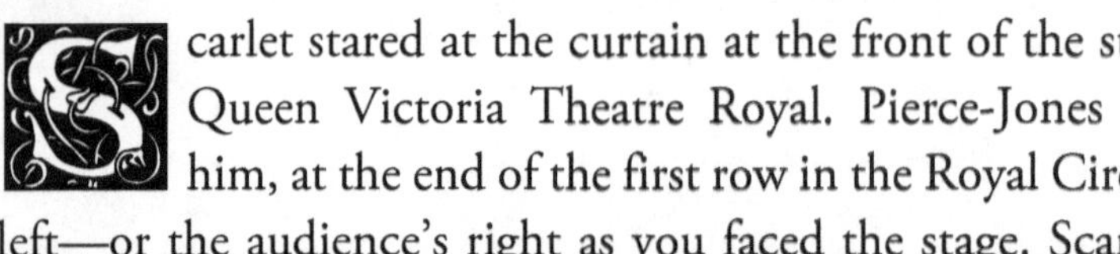carlet stared at the curtain at the front of the stage in the Queen Victoria Theatre Royal. Pierce-Jones sat beside him, at the end of the first row in the Royal Circle at stage left—or the audience's right as you faced the stage. Scarlet was in the last seat in the row, just a few strides from the exit door.

From these seats in the first balcony, they had a superb view. They would be able to see what was happening on stage from close-up, with no difficulties caused by bad sight-lines or too much distance. From the exit door close at hand, Scarlet estimated he could be on the stage itself in less than a minute—perhaps considerably less.

The drop bore the legend SAFETY CURTAIN, in large letters written on a painted scroll. Above the words, three naked Cupid-looking angels with long curly blonde hair and tiny wings cavorted, waving garlands and feathers. Also painted on the curtain were Greek or Roman columns set into a fanciful architrave or molding, with Queen Victoria's crown depicted in gold at top-center. A rose-pink color wash covered the rest of the flame-proof fabric.

To Scarlet, the curtain was as innocent as the *Phantasmagoria* show they were about to see was evil. Everything he had learned about The Master of Illusion and his show since he and Django had watched it had darkened his view of the man and his magic.

Indeed, he believed that the stakes tonight couldn't be higher.

He was convinced that a woman's life was at stake, in a way that was linked to an illusion that had to be impossible to pull off. The dead could not be brought back to life, even if you were the one who had taken away those lives in the first place.

If he was right, Catherine was going to be made to participate in 'Your Fondest Wish'. He didn't know exactly how, but he believed it would be as a human sacrifice, just as in the civilizations von Leiden mentioned and even called up through his magic. That fact had obliterated his interest in how this magician could keep his promise of producing all the former volunteers in his famous trick, whom Scarlet knew were all dead.

Unfortunately, until events started to unfold, the cards were all in von Leiden's hands. He, Django, and the force would not be able to act, but only *react* to whatever happened on stage.

Given the situation, they were as prepared as they could be. The Metropolitan Police had the building surrounded, with heavily armed officers standing by with patrol wagons on Suffolk Street behind the theatre. Detectives in plain clothes were among the standing-room-only patrons at the back of the stalls; and uniformed officers were waiting discreetly at every exit out of view from the stage floor. The House Manager had been briefed on the Yard's deployment and demands for the evening. Once the doors at the back of the house had been closed—as they were being closed now—no one would be allowed it to leave the theatre for any reason whatsoever.

The curtain rose on the final London performance of the 1888-1889 season of "Max von Leiden: The Master of Illusion's *Phantasmagoria*."

The first half of the show seemed to go by in minutes. All of von Leiden's signature illusions were there—the bare stage and the rude table on which he turned wine into water; the electrical storm which couldn't harm the audience volunteers inside the circle under von Leiden "protection"; the five male volunteers changed into creatures with swine heads and back again; the small crocodile wax figure which became seven feet long and devoured a woman; and to close the act once again, the summoning of the Mesopotamian goddess Ninlil.

In other circumstances, Scarlet might have watched each of these illusions a second time with more attention as to how they were accomplished. But not tonight. His emotions were at too high a pitch. He endured the first half of the show and the interval as best he could, waiting for the opening of the second act. The excitement of the patrons around him was equally palpable, as everyone eagerly awaited *Phantasmagoria's* grand finale featuring the season-ending 'Your Fondest Wish' illusion.

The public didn't know, of course, that all of the previous volunteers were victims of the Methuselah Plague. If Scarlet hadn't been able to share that knowledge with Mallinson and the Yard, how could he have released it to the public? Not only would he be thought mad; but the panic that would follow at the news of a modern-day necromancer would be unstoppable. He could almost see the mobs burning magicians at the stake in front of the Houses of Parliament.

THE SECOND ACT OF *Phantasmagoria* opened the same way it had in May at the performance Scarlet and Pierce-Jones had attended.

The rising curtain revealed a stage dominated by the same light-blue scrim. Once again, the audience would be able to observe what took place behind the thin fabric when the gas lights above the stage were lit. As before, the small area between the front of the scrim and the edge of the stage—which was perhaps twenty feet deep—was empty. As Scarlet knew, this was where Max von Leiden and the audience volunteer would stand as he put that person into a mesmeric trance.

Again, the audience applauded as soon as the rising curtain revealed the setting for 'Your Fondest Wish.' And just as before, only after the applause had died down and the moment of drama had built did von Leiden stride from the wings, until he stood center-stage on the narrow apron of space available to him.

As he did at the performance in May, he addressed his audience:

"Ladies and gentlemen: welcome to the world of 'Your Fondest Wish,' where all things are possible! Tonight, at the mere cost of your ticket, you will watch a miracle occur. 'Your Fondest Wish'—where illusions are reality, and where time is suspended! Where your past becomes your future! And where the world you thought you knew vanishes before your very eyes!"

Scarlet glanced to his left at the other patrons in the row. He could see that they were already mesmerized—and without a single pass having been performed yet by Herr von Leiden! The magician already seemed to have succeeded in making an illusion a reality. He continued to weave his magical tapestry:

"Here, in this theatre, I will prove that you are responsible for your own destiny!"

[Strong applause]

"Are you ready to throw off the chains of the lie of divine will? Will you dare to think and act for yourself—and so turn your own life into a miracle? DO YOU BELIEVE THAT TO CONTROL THE FUTURE, YOU ONLY HAVE TO WISH FOR IT?"

The powerful voice energized the crowd like an electric shock. They leaped to their feet, shouting and applauding as if spellbound.

Once more, von Leiden waited for the noise to subside. Then he delivered the news that none of the wild-eyed audience members could have anticipated. His excited voice perfectly captured the passion and magnitude of the moment and event.

"For the one and only time—AT THIS PERFORMANCE—you will ALL have the opportunity to be mesmerized and experience the true nature of 'Your Fondest Wish'!"

Shouting and expressions of delight greeted this unexpected news.

"But first, as I promised you, all of the volunteers from this season are with us tonight. They are ready to share with you how their most heartfelt wishes have come true!"

The flames on the upstage gaslights dimmed, turned lower by an unseen hand, and a world of deep blue moonlight became visible behind the scrim. From the very back of that area, as if being raised from a lower level, appeared a group of people that the lighting effect outlined only in silhouette. Scarlet counted thirty-five figures, spread out now in a wide line behind the scrim.

The semi-darkness of the upstage area, and the distance from there to the nearest seats in the house, meant that these people couldn't be made out clearly. They remained dark human silhouettes. But the stage in front of the scrim was still well-lit. If the figures walked forward into the light, their faces—and therefore their identities—would become known.

The Master of Illusion played the moment for all it was worth.

"But before our past participants share their extraordinary experiences with you, my friends, I would like to share a very special part of our show. First, then—we are delighted to introduce tonight's volunteer!"

Von Leiden made a gesture toward stage left. Two female assistants immediately appeared from the wings, each lightly holding onto one arm of the woman they were leading on stage.

It was Catherine Wilson. She walked toward von Leiden in a slow shuffle, exhibiting the look and gait of someone who has been drugged.

"This young lady has graciously volunteered to join our roster of 'Your Fondest Wish' participants. In a moment you will witness—"

But Scarlet didn't hear the rest. He had crashed through the swing doors at the end of the aisle and was now sprinting along the corridor toward the stairs. Then he was through the identical swing doors one floor below. He was in the house again, this time in the first-floor stalls rather than the Royal Circle one level above. Only seven rows of blue-upholstered seats now separated him from the stage. He hadn't altered his momentum as he came through the doors—hadn't stopped running—so he made short work of the aisle and was now leaping onto the four-foot high stage seemingly without effort.

The expression on von Leiden's face when Scarlet leaped onto the stage was half surprise, half amusement. He turned with the grace of a ballet dancer and disappeared around the edge of the scrim to his right. As he ran, he waved his right arm—a sweeping movement that ended with a flick upward—toward the line of silhouetted people behind the scrim. Scarlet's gaze swung toward the area of blue moonlight and he saw that the thirty-five human figures had now become ambulatory, and were walking slowly toward the light.

Ahead of him, he saw von Leiden stop suddenly. The magician must have realized that he could go no farther. The edge of the scrim ended at a masking curtain hanging inches from a brick wall. Scarlet was now positioned between the magician and his only other means of exit: the offstage area to the right. The two stood stock-still, facing each other.

"I could crush you," said von Leiden, his voice calm and cold.

"Like you did to Roach?"

The other grinned. "Perfect name, wasn't it? Yes, like I did to the roach."

"Why don't you?"

"Ah. That would spoil my image with my admirers tonight, wouldn't it? All that business about free will and determining your own fate."

"Your admirers?"

"Of course. What do you think they are? They admire me and live their lives according to my principles. Hence, all of this." To Scarlet, his gesture indicated not the theatre around them, but the wider world.

"That's a lie—though everything about you is a lie, isn't it? The people out there tonight don't live by your principles. They're just human beings who fail from time to time, however hard they try not to."

Von Leiden seemed to enjoy that thought.

"Yes, they do, don't they? But you see, they live in *my* world: the one made up of lies and illusions. Which is just what they're made for. All I do is show them the path. They go down it willingly on their own, and enjoy every step along the way."

"You are the devil, then?"

Von Leiden laughed heartily.

"Haven't you heard, Dr. William Scarlet? I'm The Master of Illusion. . . . Or am I really a demon—or perhaps Satan himself?"

"I understand why you lied to people about their fondest wish. But why did you kill them in that way, making them age rapidly and then die?"

"The Methuselah Plague! What a delightful name your people have given the affliction. But was that really me? Or haven't you heard about the old, old bargain, where you sell your soul to get what you desire but then have to pay the consequences? These people made their deals. They may not have had to sign a scroll with their blood, but they made them nevertheless. Why should anyone mourn them?"

"That is just your cruelty speaking."

". . . Which for me is merely another word for pleasure."

While this dialogue had been going on, Scarlet had been studying angles and distances, wondering if he could intercept the being opposite him if it tried to flee.

"What now, Herr von Leiden, or whatever your real name is?"

"Why, my blessing, of course!"

The Master of Illusion held out his hands in the way of a benediction, a look of mocking sadness and piety on his sharp features. Then he smiled. The eyes were piercing and malignant again. His right hand made a sweeping gesture toward the floor in front of where he was standing.

A whisp of white smoke began rising there. It quickly billowed outward: a cloud between the two of them that changed color rapidly—from red to purple to green to yellow. When it dissipated just seconds later, von Leiden was gone. Scarlet thought he heard an echo of mocking laughter, but decided he was imagining it.

Apparently, the stage magician's vanishing trick was too good to pass up.

Scarlet ran to the front of the stage. Catherine's eyes had opened, but they were fluttering, and he caught her as she fainted. He heard a collective gasp from the audience. He turned around just in time to see the silhouetted figures from 'Your Fondest Wish,' who had been walking toward the lighted part of the stage, finish fading from view.

Entry from the *Voight-Lang Enzyklopädie*

Maximilian von Leiden
German magician
Known as Max von Leiden

Born: 1851 (month and date unknown), Marburg, Germany
Died(?): July 6, 1889, London, England

Maximilian von Leiden was a German magician who was considered one of the leading conjurers of late nineteenth-century Europe. Performing as "Max von Leiden: The Master of Illusion," he invented the electrical storm trick (which was copied and adapted by many other magicians). He is most famous for 'Your Fondest Wish,' an onstage illusion which purportedly told the future of audience volunteers as well as their past.

He was known for utilizing a style of "dark magic" which relied heavily on mesmerism (a style of hypnotism popular at the time), psychological insights, and sometimes on-stage cruelty. As Leonhard Wessell points out in his book, *Bühnenillusionen und Wahnvorstellungen* (*Stage Illusions and Delusions*, Knebel & Co., Berlin, 1905), "Maximilian von Leiden" translates in English to "maximum from suffering." Max von Leiden disappeared during the finale of his show *Phantasmagoria* at the Queen Victoria Theatre Royal in London on the evening of July 6, 1889. He was never seen or heard from again, and his body was never found.

If you liked *The Master of Illusion*, please consider contributing a review on Amazon or wherever you bought the book.

Ready for more supernatural suspense? Follow Dr. Scarlet and Django Pierce-Jones in all their investigations! You'll find all of the books in the Dr. William Scarlet Mystery Series at www.garygenard.com.

GARY GENARD is the author of the Dr. William Scarlet mysteries. He lives in Massachusetts. You can find his fiction and nonfiction books at www.garygenard.com.